Praise for the Raine Stockton Dog Mystery Series

"An exciting, original and suspense-laden whodunit... A simply fabulous mystery starring a likeable, dedicated heroine..."
   --*Midwest Book Review*

"A delightful protagonist...a well-crafted mystery."
--*Romantic Times*

"There can't be too many golden retrievers in mystery fiction for my taste."
   --*Deadly Pleasures*

" An intriguing heroine, a twisty tale, a riveting finale, and a golden retriever to die for. [This book] will delight mystery fans and enchant dog lovers."
   ---*Carolyn Hart*

"Has everything--wonderful characters, surprising twists, great dialogue. Donna Ball knows dogs, knows the Smoky Mountains, and knows how to write a page turner. I loved it."
   --*Beverly Connor*

"Very entertaining... combines a likeable heroine and a fascinating mystery... a story of suspense with humor and tenderness."

   --*Carlene Thompson*

The Raine Stockton Dog Mystery series books in order:

Smoky Mountain Tracks
Rapid Fire
Gun Shy
Bone Yard (a novella)
Silent Night
The Dead Season
High in Trial
(All that Glitters: a Christmas short story)
Double Dog Dare
Home of the Brave
Dog Days

Also by Donna Ball:

FLASH
Book One in the Dogleg Island Mystery Series

DOG DAYS

A Raine Stockton Dog Mystery Book #10

By Donna Ball

Published by Blue Merle Publishing
Drawer H
Mountain City, Georgia 30562
www.bluemerlepublishing.com
ISBN: 0996561005
9780996561006

First printing July 2015

This is a work of fiction. All places, characters, events and organizations mentioned in this book are either the product of the author's imagination, or used fictitiously.

Cover art by www.bigstock.com

CHAPTER ONE

When I think back on that awful week, and particularly on how it ended, what I remember most is not the murder, or the whole horrible mess with Miles, or even the beautiful dog who wandered into my life that sweltering August morning. What I remember is the heat.

A lot of people don't think it gets hot here in the heart of the Smoky Mountains, which is why this is where they come when they want to get *away* from the heat. The truth is we see our share of ninety-degree days here every summer, but I've got to admit, I couldn't recall a stretch quite this hot, or this long, in years. Of course, we are talking about the dog days of summer, here: those long, hot, lazy days of July and August when heat waves ripple off the asphalt and dusty wildflowers droop in the sunshine by the side of the road. Smart dogs crawl under the porch and lie panting in the shade until sunset, and smart people grab a piece of real estate in the middle of one of the cold clear streams that tumble through this part of the

Smokies, add a six pack and an inner tube, and settle in for the duration. August is the time for porch swings and county fairs, cold suppers and bright still afternoons in which your main ambition is to move as little as possible. By August, everyone is tired of summer, tired of the heat, and ready to get out of town.

But when you live in a vacation destination like Hansonville and own the only dog boarding, training, and grooming facility within a hundred miles, the term dog days takes on a whole new meaning. This, after all, is where all those people who want to get out of town in August *go*, crowding up our scenic highways with RVs, minivans, and motorcycle caravans, double-parking on our streets, filling up our restaurants, and complaining about the high-fat content of our home-style meals; snapping selfies before our sweeping vistas and exclaiming over our "quaint" mountain arts and crafts. August is also the time of year when all the locals who can afford to do so make it a point to be somewhere else, and whether they are coming in or going out, when it comes to caring for the family pet, everyone turns to me.

My name is Raine Stockton, and I own the aforementioned boarding, training, and grooming facility whose name just happens to be, well, Dog Daze. Currently, I can accommodate twenty overnight boarders, five or six in day care, and eight dogs a day for grooming, and in August we are always full. I teach two obedience classes a week, plus Monday morning puppy kindergarten and two rounds of agility on Saturdays—when I'm not off competing somewhere myself, of course. I'm also the president and sole volunteer of Mountain Golden Retriever Rescue, the local contact person for the Western North Carolina chapter of Purebred Rescue, and a member of the board of the Hanover County Humane Society, for which I had volunteered to man a booth at the county fair Saturday afternoon, as soon as I finished judging the 4-H dog show, of course.

To make matters even more hectic, in addition to my own three fantastic dogs—Cisco, Mischief, and Magic—I happened to be pet-sitting Pepper, who belongs to my boyfriend Miles's daughter, one of the people I love most in the world. What I mean to say is that Melanie is one of the people I love most in the world; it's entirely possible Miles might be as well, but since I'd barely gotten more than a five-word text from him since the two of them left for Brazil over a week ago, how would I know? I heard from Melanie every day, though, mostly photos of her mom, her dad, and herself at the beach, or around the pool, or in some funky outdoor cafe. Did I mention that her mother lives in Brazil? That would be Miles's ex-wife. The one with the gorgeous tan and the bikini that you have to squint your eyes to see. The one he was at the beach with. Right now.

Pepper was doing great, though. She's wild about my golden retriever, Cisco, who tolerates her hero-worship with good-natured indulgence, and she, by the same token, tolerates my Aussies Mischief and Magic, who steal her toys and hide them and always push her to the back of the line at treat time. The four of them were in my office now, secured by an exercise pen, happily barking their heads off. This meant that all the other dogs up and down the kennel corridor were also barking like wild hounds on a full moon, and the pop music that blared from the playroom didn't help. To me it was all just comfortable background noise, but I could see how someone else might find it a little chaotic. That was probably why my friend Sonny couldn't resist pointing out to me, for what must have been the fifth time in the past hour, that I really needed to hire some help.

"I have help," I returned, a little defensively. I was putting the finishing touches on her border collie, Mystery, a working sheep dog who had had an unfortunate encounter with a muddy creek and a lot of sheep poop that morning and who was growing visibly impatient on the grooming table as I worked the slicker brush through her now shiny, sweet-smelling fur. "The kids are working out great."

That might have been an exaggeration. I had hired two part-time high school girls for the summer; they were supposed to be full time, but since they only worked when they didn't have anything better to do, part time was what I got. For example, at that moment, Katie and Marilee were having a great time playing with the dogs in the day care room while Taylor Swift blared in the background, but when it came time to clean the kennels they would suddenly remember they'd promised to pick up their little sisters or weed the garden for their moms.

"Besides," I added, "I'm interviewing people. I have someone coming in this afternoon."

"Hire her," Sonny advised sternly.

"It's a him."

"Hire him," she repeated.

"It's not that easy. I can't just turn my business over to anyone. He has to have training, education, experience, references, a background check. Then there's an internship period, and a probationary period—"

Sonny pointed out dryly, "You forgot the oral and written exams."

I scowled at her.

"Seriously, Raine, don't you think your standards might be just a tad high? Where are you going to find someone like that around here?"

"I have a reputation to uphold. People trust me with their dogs. I have to be careful."

Mystery gave a sudden impatient bark and Sonny rolled her eyes. "I quite agree, Mystery," she said.

Without giving me a chance to ask what it was that she agreed with Mystery about—not that I would have, anyway—she changed the subject. "Are you sure you don't want me to take your place at the Humane Society booth? I don't mind, and Hero always draws a crowd."

In addition to being a fairly well-known environmental attorney, Sonny was an animal rights advocate who had established a small animal sanctuary on her property not far from town. She wasn't much over fifty, but degenerative rheumatoid arthritis had limited her mobility, and Hero was her service dog, a somber yellow lab who took his job very seriously. He was stretched out at Sonny's feet now, and was the only dog in the building who hadn't barked once in the past hour.

To show him my appreciation, I took a treat from the big jar I kept by the grooming table and tossed it to him. He caught it in midair and swallowed it in a single gulp. Mystery gave me an accusing look, so I gave her a treat as well which she munched on while I combed out the last tangle behind her ear. "Thanks, but you've already signed up for Friday, and I don't mind. I have to be there anyway for the dog show, and I'm going to take Cisco."

I loved our little county fair, which we worked hard to keep as pure and old fashioned as we could. There was a Ferris wheel and a tilt-a-whirl, carnival games and agricultural shows, bluegrass music and jam judging. I had looked forward to attending it this year with Miles and Melanie, but it was not to be, and I was a little bummed about that. The fact that I had barely heard from Miles at all since he'd been gone had nothing to do with that.

I gave Mystery a final fluff and a quick kiss on the nose, then unfastened the grooming harness. "Okay girl, you're ready to go." Three down, five to go.

"Thanks, Raine." Using a cane to steady herself, Sonny got to her feet. "I wish you'd let me pay you." Hero rose without a command and leaned in to steady her.

I waved a dismissing hand. "Don't be silly. She's—"

But before I could finish that sentence, the dog I'd been about to describe as "no trouble at all" sprang off the grooming table, skidded across the linoleum floor, course-corrected, and zoomed through the door. Sonny gave an exclamation of dismay, and I raced after her, not because I was afraid she'd escape the building, which was sealed tight, but because I knew exactly where she was going. I was right.

I arrived just in time to see Mystery launch herself with playful exuberance toward the ex-pen, encouraging her best buddies, Mischief and Magic, to show off their favorite trick. First one and then the other Australian shepherd sprang from a flat-footed bounce over the top of the forty-eight-inch-tall wire fence, grinning like the wicked angels they were. Unfortunately, when Cisco tried the same thing, he forgot that golden retrievers are twice the size and perhaps one-third as agile as Aussies. His back foot got caught in a wire panel, sending the entire pen toppling over to a chorus of yips and barks and some rather alarmed shrieking from Pepper, who had a tendency to overdramatize these things.

Dogs scurried away in a tangle of paws and tails. I dived to catch the ring leader, who at this point was Cisco, and overturned a box of tennis balls in the process. Cisco immediately raced after one bouncing ball, Pepper dashed through my legs after another, and my feet went out from under me. I grabbed for a shelf to stop my fall and overturned another box. I landed hard on my rear just as two hundred fifty dog biscuits scattered across the floor.

"We're okay!" I called out, and by the time Sonny arrived, we were. All five dogs had lost interest in whatever mayhem they had been planning and were busily gobbling down dog biscuits. I hauled myself upright and started sweeping up dog biscuits and orange tennis balls with my hands. Sonny commanded sharply from the door, "Mystery, come here."

Mystery dropped the biscuit that was in her mouth and raced to Sonny's side. I gave Sonny a dry look over my shoulder. She couldn't have done that *before* Mystery reached my office?

"Oh, Raine," Sonny said, her tone dismayed. "What a mess. Do you need any help?"

I dumped an armful of tennis balls and dog biscuits into a box. "Just another morning at Dog Daze," I said.

I caught Pepper's collar with one hand and righted the ex-pen with the other, ushering her inside and latching the gate firmly. The Aussies, who had started the whole fray, I consigned to their crates in opposite corners of the room. I was just about to deal with Cisco when I heard a car horn blasting from outside.

"Oh dear," Sonny said, "another customer. Raine, seriously, you have got to …"

"That's not a customer," I said, peering through the window. "That's Rick."

Rick was my boss—former boss, I should say, since budget cuts meant that I had been regulated to "off the payroll but valued volunteer" status—at the Forest Service. He was driving a green forest service pickup truck, and he wasn't alone in the cab, which was why I grabbed a slip leash and hurried out of the office almost before I finished speaking. Cisco, thinking I'd forgotten about him, trotted happily along at my side, but I put him in a down-stay on the paw-print-painted walkway as soon as we got outside, and closed the gate firmly. Sonny followed closely behind with Mystery and Hero.

"Hey, Raine," Rick called as he got out of the truck.

"Hey, yourself," I replied. "What've you got?"

He started around to the passenger door, but already I could see the beautiful golden head regarding us all through the windshield, assessing the situation with a calm and regal gaze. "We picked her up a couple of hours ago on the west ridge of Hemlock Mountain," Rick said. "She's got a collar, but no tags, looks like she's been running loose for a while. We sent out notices to all the campsites, but until somebody claims her, I was wondering if you could ..."

However he finished that sentence was lost in my own soft exclamation of wonder. "Oh, my! It's an English Cream golden!"

Actually, the term "English Cream" is something of a misnomer, since all golden retrievers, if traced back to their origin, have British ancestry, and since what we call English Cream goldens really bear little resemblance to the British standard golden retriever at all. Their lustrous cream-colored coat is somewhat unique in this part of the world, and, until a few years ago, might even be called rare. Until now, I had never seen one in person outside a major breed specialty show.

"She's kind of a mess," Rick apologized as he opened the door. "Who knows how long she's been running loose, or what she got into. Looks like dried mud all over her fur."

I edged past Rick, crooning softly, "Hello there, gorgeous." She regarded me impassively from the front seat of the truck, her deep brown eyes revealing nothing. I stroked her head, easing the loop of the leash around her neck. "What a sweet, beautiful girl."

Of course, at the moment, she wasn't particularly beautiful. Her fur was tangled with leaves and dried twigs, and her chest and belly were stiff with dried mud, as though she'd slept in a mud puddle. I ran my fingers gently through the crusty coat around her throat, trying to work out some of the layers of mud that coated her fur. My Dog Daze tee shirt was still splotched with wet spots from washing Mystery, and when I brushed against the golden, the specks of mud in her coat melted, leaving streaks of red on the damp fabric.

I looked at my shirt, frowning, then turned back to the dog. I worked more of the crusty substance on her fur between my fingers. I looked at Rick worriedly. "That's not mud," I said. "It's blood."

CHAPTER TWO

Rick said, "She didn't look hurt when I found her. I guess she might've killed something, but ..." He gave a small shake of his head. "It would've had to be a mighty big animal to bleed that much. Deer, maybe?"

Sonny started toward us. "Raine? Do you need help?"

I replied over my shoulder, "No thanks, Sonny. Better not bring the dogs any closer, though. We don't want any incidents."

Sonny promised to call me later, and put the dogs in her car. As she drove away, I turned back to the golden, stroking her ears. "I never heard of a golden bringing down a deer," I said to Rick. "Have you?"

He admitted it didn't seem likely.

"She might have some injury we can't see," I said. "I'll have the vet check her out. I can't put her in with the other dogs until she has her shots anyway. Meantime, if anybody calls about her, tell them I've got her. I'll stop by the sheriff's office and let them know, and put an announcement on the radio."

"Thanks, Raine." He glanced around. "Looks like you're staying busy."

I knew he felt bad about having to let me go, but it wasn't his fault the government cut his budget, so I tried not to rub it in. "Business couldn't be better," I assured him. "You know how it is this time of year."

"Boy, do I ever." He took off his hat and ran his fingers through his sweaty, plastered-down hair. "I sure could use you back on the team, but the way things are ..." Again he looked embarrassed and regretful.

"I know," I said. "But it probably worked out for the best. I can hardly keep up with all I've got going on here." As I spoke I kept a reassuring hand on the golden's collar, rubbing her jaw with the other. She relaxed, stretching out her paws on the front seat.

"Looks like it. Well, I gotta get back. I'll let you know if I hear anything on the dog."

"Same here. Be sure to tell everybody hey for me, okay?"

"Will do."

He started around to the driver's side of the truck and I gave a gentle tug on the leash. "Come on, sweetie, let's go." To my relief, the dog jumped out of the truck without any further urging. Sometimes these things can be a struggle.

I turned to lead her away as Rick made the three-point turn to leave, and that was when I noticed that Cisco had not only broken his down-stay, but was standing with his paws on the fence, grinning like a fool at the new dog. "Cisco!" I said sternly, careful not to sound so threatening that I would spook the new dog. "Shame on you! Where do you belong?"

Cisco is a smart dog and, I like to think, very well trained. After all, he is a Canine Good Citizen, a registered therapy dog, certified in Level Two Wilderness Search and Rescue, and holds titles in both Novice and Open agility. Of course, he's never won an obedience title, possibly because, while he knows all the commands, he tends to use his own judgment when deciding whether or not to execute them. But my "Shame on you!" voice almost always works with him, and the only reason I could think of that he wasn't responding to it now was because I hadn't been tough enough.

I rested a soothing hand on the golden's head and murmured, "Sorry, sweetheart." Then, in my not-to-be-ignored voice, I shouted, "Cisco, *down*!"

To my surprise, the golden beside me immediately dropped to a down. I murmured, "Oh my!" and quickly dug into my pocket for a treat. The golden licked it up while I praised her for the good dog she was, and Cisco barked, wagging his tail frantically, his paws clawing at the fence.

I stared at Cisco sternly, and the sweet golden at my side did not move. After a moment Cisco reluctantly stretched into a down, his tail still swishing on the concrete walkway, his grin broad enough to melt the coldest heart. I actually had to compress my lips to keep from smiling back as I reached into a pocket for a treat. "Okay, you rascal."

I approached the fence to toss him his treat, the new dog walking politely at my side. But we hadn't gone three feet before Cisco bounded up again, paws on the fence, yipping like a puppy with excitement. Having worked with dogs most of my life, I know that they not only recognize, but often prefer, members of their own breed, so of course Cisco was happy to see another golden. But dozens of goldens come through here every year and he should definitely be used to it by now. As far as I was concerned, this behavior was inexcusable. I spun on my heel and walked the other way.

Shunning, in dog language, is a fairly effective treatment for a deliberately disobedient dog. The next time your dog is flinging himself at you uncontrollably when you come home, try turning your back on him, crossing your arms, and refusing to make eye contact. It won't take long before he figures out he has done something wrong. And of course a tried and true method for getting the attention of a dog who refuses to come when you call is to simply walk away. If there's a gate you can shut between you and him, or a car you can get in that he can't, so much the better. You'd be amazed at how much bad-dog bravado goes out of a dog when he's ignored and left behind.

Sad to say, Cisco has been the recipient of this kind of disapproval more than once, and he responded immediately by remembering what he'd done wrong and sinking reluctantly into the down-stay once again. This did not surprise me, although I'll admit a certain sense of gratification. What did surprise me was that the golden kept perfect pace with my fierce, determined stride. Someone had definitely put some time into training this dog.

I crossed the driveway that separated Dog Daze from my house and put the golden in the chain-link run I designated for rescues. As much as I would have liked to bathe and spiff her up myself, my rule is hard-and-fast: no rescues come into contact with other dogs until they've been vetted. We'd had a bad outbreak of parvo this summer, and leptospirosis was making a comeback in the mountains, not to mention canine flu. With a full kennel, there was no way I was taking a chance.

I called the vet on my way to release Cisco from his down-stay, and his receptionist—also his wife—said that if I could get the golden in within the hour, they could see her right away. The minute I hung up, Melanie called. The child was calling from Brazil. Of course I took the call.

"Hey, Mel," I answered happily. "What's up?" I opened the gate and gave Cisco a treat for maintaining his stay until I returned. Then, and only then, did I give him the hand signal for "release." He bounded to his feet and began to sniff my legs, my shoes, anywhere the other dog had touched.

"Hey, Raine!" she replied. "How's Pepper?"

"Perfect," I assured her. I snapped my fingers and Cisco fell into heel position beside me as we walked back to the kennel building. Too bad he couldn't demonstrate that level of obedience when it counted. "She was the demo dog in puppy class yesterday, and all the other dogs were so jealous. Afterward we all went out for doggie fro-yo. Pepper paid, of course."

Melanie giggled. "Hope she didn't forget the tip."

"No chance." I opened the door to the building and gestured Cisco inside. I remained outside, where I could actually have a telephone conversation without the deafening cacophony of barking. "What about you? Are you having fun?"

"Oh, sure," she replied, somewhat distractedly. "Lots of culturally significant stuff. Museums, galleries, you know. Say, Raine." She lowered her voice conspiratorially, and even over the thousands of miles that separated us, I could hear the undertone of excitement. "There's news."

"Yeah? Can't wait."

"Well." She took an important breath, then blurted, "My mom is getting a divorce from her new husband. That means she doesn't have to live in Brazil anymore! That means she can live in the States and I can see her any time I want! Maybe she'll even move to North Carolina!"

I felt as though I'd been sucker-punched. Miles's ex-wife, the mother of his child, had been a shadowy background figure for as long as I'd known Miles. Out of country, out of mind. Married to someone else. A non-entity. And now, suddenly, she wasn't. She was real, she was sexy, she was free. And she could be moving next door.

It was a moment or two before I could actually find my breath. "Wow, Melanie," I managed. "That's huge."

"I know, right?" Her voice was practically bubbling with excitement. "Now Pepper and I don't have to worry about learning Spanish or moving or anything. Oh!" she added, on a breath. "And Mom says I can have my ears pierced! Can't wait for you to see. I'm going to get dog bone earrings like yours." She paused thoughtfully. "Maybe I'll get my belly button pierced while I'm at it."

Despite my distraction, I almost choked on a laugh. "I double-dog dare you to tell your dad that."

"Well," she admitted, "it did take a pretty long time to get him onboard with the ears. Maybe I won't tell him."

"Maybe you won't do it."

I could almost see her grin. "Probably not. Anyway, gotta go. I just wanted to tell you."

"Glad you did." I forced heartiness I was far from feeling. "Hey, Melanie, do me a favor, will you? Tell your dad to call me when he gets a chance."

"Okay, I will. And give Pepper a big hug, okay? Tell her I'll be home soon."

"Sure thing. She's sending you big doggie kisses."

She giggled again. "Bye, Raine."

After she disconnected, I took three deep breaths, and then, because I was afraid I'd lose my nerve if I waited any longer, I dialed Miles's number. It went straight to voice mail, which meant that either his phone was off—unlikely, if I knew Miles—or he'd rejected my call. I fought the impulse to hang up, waited for the tone, then said, as casually as I possibly could, "Hey, it's me. Just wondering how things are going. Call me, okay?" I hesitated, thought about adding more, and changed my mind. I finished lamely, "Bye." And hung up, wincing in embarrassment at my own ineptitude.

But I didn't have time to stand there feeling stupid. I released the two Aussies and ushered them, along with Cisco, out into the play yard. Then I stopped by the day care room and told Katie and Marilee I'd be out for a couple of hours. "Just let the phone go to voice mail," I said. "But watch the front door. Mrs. Kellerman is dropping Peaches by for her bath at 1:00. If I'm not back by then, just put her in the kennel in the grooming room. My dogs are in the play yard. You can take this crew …" I indicated the collie mix, the poodle, the two Labs, and the beagle who were milling around my feet and shoving in for petting, "out to run for a while but bring them all in after fifteen minutes. I don't want them to get too hot. And dry them off before you bring them back in." I kept wading pools scattered around the play yard this time of year, and few dogs could resist plopping down in one at least once during their run.

"Yes, ma'am," they chorused, gathering up leashes and squeaky toys.

Again I winced. No woman in her thirties likes being called ma'am. But my mother would've skinned me alive if I'd called an employer anything else besides "ma'am" or "sir" when I was their age, so I supposed I should be grateful for the respect.

"I've got my cell phone," I reminded them. "Call me if you need anything at all."

They assured me, once again with a chorus of "ma'ams," that they would as I hurried back to the house.

I stripped off my dirty clothes, showered off the dog hair, and stepped into a clean pair of white shorts and a print blouse three minutes later. I ran my fingers through my short, curly hair, knowing it would probably dry before I reached the car, grabbed my purse and a leash, and was on my way.

~*~

My relationship with Doc Witherspoon goes back fifteen years, at least, to the time I got my first golden retriever. I'd carried sick or injured dogs into his office at three a.m. and he'd been as calm and professional as he was on a well-puppy check-up at three in the afternoon. He always gave me a break on rescue dogs, charging me only anesthesia costs for spay/neuters and giving the shots for free. If you ever consider going into rescue work, it's essential to find a vet like that.

"Looks to be about four years old," he pronounced after his initial examination. "Spayed, clean ears and teeth. Good weight, nice coat. Looks like somebody took care of this dog."

"I think so too," I said. "She's very well behaved. She might even have some formal obedience training. She reminds me a lot of Hero, actually."

Hero, Sonny's service dog, had started out as a rescue much like this golden—except that we knew who his owner, unfortunately deceased, had been. He had continually amazed me with his skills until we tracked him back to the service dog organization that had trained him. Sometimes, in this business, you really do find gold.

Doc said, "Well, let's see if she has a microchip." As he turned to get the scanner, I draped an arm around the golden, holding her still on the metal table, stroking her filthy fur. She panted a little, but seemed otherwise unperturbed.

"What about the blood on her fur?"

"I don't see anything, but I'll take a closer look after we get her cleaned up. Could be a closed wound and we don't want it to abscess." He ran the scanner across her shoulder and it beeped. "There you go." He showed the screen to me. "She's chipped. I'll get Crystal to run it down for you. We might even be able to get in touch with her vet. If we can't, do you want me to go ahead and give her the full spectrum?"

I hate to over-vaccinate dogs, but if she was going to go home with me I had no choice. "Yeah," I agreed reluctantly. "But I hope you can get her shot record."

"Why don't you go get some lunch and stop back by in ..." He glanced at the clock on the wall. "Say an hour and a half? Unless something unusual shows up, she should be ready to go."

He unsnapped her collar and gave it to me. It was a little smudged and dirty, but definitely one of the high-end brands: petal pink dyed leather studded with rhinestones. Someone had treasured this dog. Then why had they been stupid enough to let her get lost in the woods?

Doc read my thoughts. "There's no accounting for people, Raine."

I sighed. "Yeah, I know. Especially city people. Thanks, Doc."

With an hour and a half to kill, I really could have gone back to work. But I had been washing dogs, walking dogs, feeding dogs, cleaning kennels, and exercising dogs since six a.m., and judging by the growling in my stomach I had forgotten to eat breakfast. I called Katie on her cell phone. She reported that all was quiet, and would it be okay if they watched the television in my office while they had their lunch? I told them to be sure to crate all the dogs and to stay off the computer and that I would be home by two at the latest. Then I drove straight to Miss Meg's diner.

Miss Meg's is an institution in Hansonville. Good solid home cooking, no Swiss chard, no radicchio, no vegan anything, and if you ask for gluten free, Miss Meg will stare you down until you slink out of the restaurant with your tail between your legs, as well you should. Her homemade buttermilk biscuits are to die for. During tourist season even locals have to fight their way to the counter for a seat, though, unless you're smart enough to dine fashionably early. Like I was.

I arrived at 11:40 and already the place was three-quarters full. Cathy, the head day waitress, picked up a menu and gestured me to follow her as soon as I entered, but I waved her off. I had already seen the K-9 unit parked outside, with Nike the Belgian Malinois, the newest member of the Hanover County Sheriff's Department, resting in air-conditioned comfort inside. Her handler, Jolene Smith, was sitting at a booth halfway down the row, finishing her lunch and reading the newspaper. I slid into the seat opposite her.

"Hey, Jolene," I said.

She took a gulp of her coffee, folded the newspaper, and started to rise.

"Oh, for crying out loud," I said, exasperated. "There's no need to be rude."

She met my gaze coolly. "I was just sitting here having my coffee. You're the one that decided to take my table."

Jolene was the first black woman ever to be hired by the Hanover County Sheriff's Department. As though that wasn't enough, she also had a fairly accomplished background as a canine handler in the military, and had done two tours in Afghanistan. This made her more qualified for the job than roughly ninety percent of the deputies on the force, and knowing those deputies as I do, I was sure it wasn't easy for her. Furthermore, her position was funded by the Department of Homeland Security, which I happened to know pissed off the sheriff. How do I know? Because Sheriff Buck Lawson is my ex-husband and, not to mince words, we're still pretty tight. After all, we'd been together since junior high.

With all that in mind, I didn't think Jolene could afford to be that particular about her friends. I knew she didn't like me, and it wasn't as though I was all that wild about her, although her dog was amazing. But we had been through some fairly intense hours together a month or so back, along with over two dozen juvenile campers and their dogs, and I just couldn't stop thinking that, because of it, we were both changed. Three fingers of her gun hand were still splinted, and her duties over the past few weeks had been mostly administrative. My wounds from that time were less visible.

I said, "Anyway, this is police business."

She cautiously eased back into her seat, but her tone was challenging. "What?"

I told her about the stray dog, and I could see her trying not to roll her eyes. "Police business?" she repeated dryly.

"This isn't New Jersey," I reminded her archly. "Around here we serve and protect, with an emphasis on the serve. This time of year a lot of people come up, camping or renting cabins, and most of them bring their dogs. They forget the dogs aren't at home and think they can just let them out to pee without a leash, and that they'll come right back like they always do. Next thing you know the dog is out after a deer, or has wandered out of hearing range and has absolutely no idea how to find his way back to his family because he's not, after all, at home. People are stupid, and dogs are the ones who suffer. But sometimes those stupid people actually have sense enough to call the sheriff's department when they lose a dog, which is why I always notify them when I find a stray. Police business." I smirked, and glanced up as Cathy arrived, order pad in hand.

"Bring me an egg salad sandwich," I said, "with sweet tea and french fries. And save me a piece of apple pie for dessert. With ice cream," I added as she hurried away, and she waved acknowledgement.

Jolene stood up. "Stop by the office and leave a report with the clerk."

I corrected, "Office manager."

"Whatever."

She walked away without saying good-bye and I called after her, "Have a good day!"

She didn't even turn around.

Cathy brought my sweet tea, made the way it was supposed to be made, with simple syrup and poured hot over ice cubes until the ice cracks and the pitcher sweats. I had just taken my first crisp, refreshing drink when a shadow fell over me and a man said, "Raine Stockton?"

He had the voice of a summons server, so naturally I tensed. But when I looked up, the face that belonged to the voice was smiling, with hazel eyes, a mustache, and curly brown hair. He couldn't have been much older than I was, and he held a glass of iced tea just like mine.

He said, by way of introduction, "Marshall Becker. Do you mind if I join you for a minute?" And, taking my speechlessness as consent, he slid into the seat that Jolene had vacated across from me. Cathy hurried to clear away the used dishes and wipe the table.

He said, as though by way of explanation, "I'm running for sheriff."

I stared at him. "I know that." It wasn't as though his picture wasn't on every telephone pole and store window in town—those not already taken by posters with pictures of the incumbent on them, of course. "Do you happen to know who you're running against?"

He smiled. "Buck Lawson, I believe is the fellow's name."

"My ex-husband," I pointed out. "You can't sit here."

"Ex being the operative word," he said. "The average person might think that's a point in my favor."

"Only if you're looking for a date," I shot back and wanted to suck the words back in as soon as they were spoken. I felt my cheeks color, and his eyes twinkled.

"Actually," he replied, "I'm looking for your vote. But it was nice of you to offer."

This time I was smart enough to keep my mouth shut—or at least to open it only long enough to take a gulp of iced tea, which cooled my burning cheeks only marginally.

He added, "Not to be too personal, but since you did bring it up … aren't you and Miles Young together? I saw you at the Chamber Awards Ceremony last month, and here and there around town. He's one of my biggest supporters."

I knew that Miles was supporting the opposition in the upcoming sheriff's election. But were we together? That I was not quite as sure about as I should have been. I said flatly, "I'm voting for Buck. And you can't sit here."

He inquired, "Why?"

Cathy brought my lunch plate—fluffy egg salad piled high between two pieces of toast topped with sliced garden tomatoes and lettuce, along with a pile of french fries that made my mouth water just looking at them. I thanked her before unwrapping my silverware from the paper napkin and returning impatiently to Marshall. "Because people are going to think exactly what Cathy did just now. That I'm friends with you. That I'm on your side, that I'm voting for you, that I'm supporting you just because Miles is. And I'm not. So go sit somewhere else."

He didn't move. "What I meant was," he clarified, "why are you voting for Buck?"

I replied in exasperation, "Because he's my hu—" This time I was able to stop myself before blurting something both stupid and humiliating, and just to make sure, I picked up a triangle of my sandwich and took a big bite. He waited patiently while I chewed, swallowed, and wiped excess mayonnaise from my lips. I tried again.

"Look," I said reasonably, "Buck is the most qualified for the job. He's been on the force longer than anyone else, he knows everybody in the county, and he was my Uncle Ro's second-in-command before he retired. He was handpicked by Uncle Ro to fill his term. Around here, we like smooth transitions. I'm voting for Buck."

He nodded. "I used to work for Sheriff Bleckley—your Uncle Ro—same as Buck. As a matter of fact, we joined the department at about the same time."

"But Buck is still here," I reminded him. "You left after five years." I stuffed a couple of french fries in my mouth and took up the sandwich again.

"To move to Tennessee," he countered, "where I worked in law enforcement for another ten years. When I came back to North Carolina I joined the state police, and I'm still a consultant there, though it's mostly part time these days." He smiled. "You ought to check out my resume. It's on my website."

If I have one fault, it's curiosity. It's gotten me into a lot more trouble than just being seen having lunch with a political candidate whose campaign I did not support ever could have done. Nonetheless, I could not resist inquiring, "So what made you come back here?"

He sipped his tea, leaning back easily. "In a way, I never left. My dad left me a couple of hundred acres along Back Ridge Creek, and I always thought I'd retire here. When my wife got sick a few years back, it seemed foolish to wait to build the dream house."

I paused with my glass midway to my lips. "You're married?"

His smile turned sad. "Unfortunately, she died before we could break ground on the house. Two years ago."

I put my glass down, murmuring, "Oh, I'm sorry."

Cathy chose that moment to stop by to refill his glass, which gave us both a moment. When she was gone he went on, "I sold most of the property—to Miles, actually—but kept a nice little parcel on the water and built a cabin. When I heard about your uncle retiring, it seemed like serendipity. Time to leave the past behind and go for the dream." He lifted his glass to me in a small salute.

I said simply, "Ah."

It was all beginning to come together for me now. Miles made his rather considerable living by turning unspoiled wilderness into high-rise condos and fly-in golf resorts. It was entirely possible that in the course of this transaction Marshall and Miles had discovered they had a shared vision for the future of Hanover County, which was why Miles was so quick to support what would have otherwise been an unpopular candidate.

I folded my hands atop the paper napkin in my lap and said, "Listen, you seem like a nice guy. But you're wasting your time with this campaign, and your money." *Miles's money,* I probably should have said, but let it go. "Buck Lawson is going to win this election. He's a hometown boy, a popular guy, and he's already been doing the job for almost a year. The people are not going to vote him out of office."

He nodded thoughtfully. "I understand. I like Buck myself, and I had to give it some thought before deciding to go up against him. But sometimes being popular is not the best qualification for a law enforcement official, even in a little place like this. Times are changing faster than most of us realize, and after what happened last month … well, the standing sheriff might not be quite as popular as you think."

I said sharply, "You can't blame Buck for that. Even the FBI didn't know what was going on until it was too late, and it was Buck who rescued the hostages and made the biggest arrest in the whole case."

Again he nodded, his expression thoughtful and oddly compassionate. "You could look at it like that, I suppose. But some people are also wondering why it ever got that far, and remembering that it was Homeland Security that actually found the bombs that could have blown up half this town."

I felt my fingertips grow cold, just with the mention of that day. He must have seen something in my face, because he added, "I don't mean to bring up unpleasant memories. But I'm running for office." Again the smile. If you could get past the mustache, it was really quite nice. "I really wish you'd go on my website and at least read my platform."

I said, "Are you going to have lunch with every voter in this county?"

And he replied, completely without guile, "You bet. That's how strongly I believe I'm the best man for the job."

I picked up my sandwich. "One down. Eight thousand, five hundred fifty-three to go."

Again he lifted his glass to me. "Nice meeting you, Raine. I hope you'll consider what I've said. I'll leave you to your lunch."

He rose and I said, "Bye," as I took another big bite of my sandwich. But to be perfectly honest, it didn't taste nearly as good as it had before I'd listened to what Marshall Becker had to say.

I had parked in the semi-shade of one of the drooping dogwoods that lined the street in front of Miss Meg's, and as I started toward my car I noticed a man standing beside it. There was nothing particularly strange about that, since every parking place on the street was taken and I figured he had just gotten out of the red sports car that was parked next to my Trailblazer. In the dead season of January or February, I would be able to walk down this same street and call every person I met by name, but this time of year the opposite was true, and the man did not look familiar at all. He was tall, a little slump-shouldered, balding on top, wearing khaki shorts and a plaid shirt with sneakers and white socks—in other words, a harmless tourist. Harmless, I thought, until he cupped his hand over his eyes and peered in the window of my SUV.

"Hey!" I said, but I was too far away for him to hear. I quickened my pace.

He walked around my car and I swear I saw him take something from his pocket—a cell phone?—and point it at the rear of my vehicle. That was strange, but it wasn't until he moved around to the driver's door and tried the handle that I started to run. "Hey!" I shouted, and heads turned. "Hey, get away from my car!"

This may be a small town full of strangers, but it's still a small town. When a woman starts running down the street screaming at a man, people stop and stare. Other men move closer to get a better look. Their wives take out their cell phones to dial 911. I could see the slump-shouldered man turn abruptly and dart his eyes around for the easiest escape route, but when you are constantly chasing after a dog as fast as Cisco, you get to be pretty fast yourself. I grabbed his arm before he could take the first sprinting step.

"What are you doing?" I demanded, breathing hard.

He jerked his arm away and raised both hands up in a placating gesture. "Lady, I don't know what your problem is—"

"You were trying to break into my car!"

He looked outraged. "What are you talking about? This is my car! I locked the keys inside, that's all."

"Oh, yeah?" I dug into my purse for my keys. "Oh yeah?"

A smooth male voice said behind me, "Is everything okay here?"

I looked up to see Marshall Becker, and though I don't usually respond well to men who like to think their main role in life is to swoop in and rescue women at the last minute, in this case I was glad for the eyewitness.

"This man was trying to break into my car!" I said indignantly.

He broke in with equal indignation, "This crazy woman ran up and grabbed me and started yelling at me just because I locked my keys in my car!"

I finally found my keys, yanked them out, and pointed the remote triumphantly at the door. The door clicked open and I tossed him a smug look as I pulled open the door and looked inside. Just in case I had any doubt, there were leashes in the door pockets, pickup bags in the cup holders, and the stray dog's pink collar on the passenger seat. "No keys," I pronounced, and turned to glare at him.

The stranger looked dismayed. "I, um, I was sure I parked here."

A woman called out, "Do you want me to call the police?"

The stranger looked panicky and Marshall called back, "Thanks, just a misunderstanding."

I turned my glare on Marshall. "Excuse me? I'm the victim here."

The man's tone took on a note of pleading as he slowly lowered his hands, "Come on, lady, an honest mistake. I'm just a regular guy passing through town on my way to the Blue Ridge Parkway. The wife and I are staying overnight at the Black Bear Lodge, you can check. My car looks just like this, same year and everything. I don't know how I could have misplaced …" He started patting his pockets, and a look of sheepish remorse came over his face as he pulled out a set of keys. "Oh," he said.

Marshall raised an eyebrow. "It's up to you. You can call the police if you want."

I snapped, "I know I can."

The man looked distressed. "Lady, please."

I rolled my shoulders irritably and waved him away. "Oh, go on."

Both Marshall and I watched him hurry across the street, head down, and turn the corner. "He was lying," I said, still scowling.

"People make mistakes," Marshall replied.

"I've got an AKC sticker on my windshield," I pointed out irritably, "and bumper stickers on the back."

"Maybe he didn't see them."

"He walked around the back. I think he took a picture."

"That is odd," Marshall admitted. And he looked at me sympathetically. "I guess after everything you've been through, you have a right to be a little paranoid."

"I am not paranoid." I scowled fiercely and pushed my fingers through my curls. "This kind of thing has happened before," I told him. "Ever since that stupid article about Cisco and me came out in *North Carolina Today*." That article, which had been picked up a few weeks later by a national news magazine, had painted Cisco—and me, I guess—as heroes in a very bad incident that had taken place over the Fourth of July. My fifteen minutes of fame had not been nearly as enjoyable as one might expect. "Reporters calling any time of the day or night, perfect strangers taking my picture on the street or driving right up to my house, people e-mailing me with messages for Cisco ... some guy even wanted to make a movie of my life. Turned out he was a twenty-two-year-old film student with a point-and-shoot. I'm just tired of it all. It's weird and it's annoying and I am not paranoid."

He nodded sympathetically, but I could tell he wasn't entirely convinced. "I'm just saying. It would be understandable if you were."

I looked at him coolly. "Men with mustaches never win elections," I said.

I got in the car and slammed the door, and I could swear he was chuckling as he watched me back out and drive away.

But the time I'd driven the four blocks to the public safety building, I was over my irritation, and I certainly wasn't going to waste anybody's time with an incident report about a confused tourist. However, it only made sense, as long as I was in town, to follow up on the stray dog, so I made the left turn onto Courthouse Square and found a parking space.

I don't spend as much time around the sheriff's office as I used to, but I'm still fairly comfortable there. Between my uncle having been sheriff for thirty years, and being married to Buck for most of my adult life—off and on, anyway—I know everyone in the department and everyone knows me. I had some time before I was due to pick up the golden, so I decided to stop by the office, as Jolene had suggested, and leave a description. Who knew? Maybe someone had already called in looking for her.

The blast of air-conditioned air felt good after the walk across the parking lot under the blaring sun. I pushed open the glass door of the sheriff's department to a burst of laughter and the sound of applause. That was my first hint that a party of some kind was going on; the second hint was the slice of frosted cake on the empty reception desk. I could see everyone was gathered in the bullpen, where a tall cake and a bowl of punch had been set up. I started toward them.

This kind of thing probably isn't procedure, but the sheriff's department is its own little family, and my uncle always believed that impromptu celebrations of things like birthdays and promotions were good for morale. Even though I had just finished a slice of pie with ice cream, I wouldn't say no to a piece of birthday cake. It looked as though it had come from the bakery, which was not something I got to have very often.

"Hi, guys," I called, pushing through the gate that separated the desks from the lobby. "Whose birthday?"

The laughter and chatter died down little by little as the deputies and employees turned to look at me, their expressions oddly embarrassed. This was about the same time I noticed that the three-tiered cake was not a birthday cake, but a wedding cake, and that the bride and groom on top were not wearing a tuxedo and wedding dress, but sheriff's department uniforms. I noticed this at the same time I noticed my ex-husband with his arm around Wyn, the only other female deputy on the force besides Jolene, and the woman Buck had left me for. They each had pieces of cake between their fingers and smears of icing on their faces, having apparently just finished feeding each other the traditional bite of wedding cake. And that was when I noticed the glittering diamond on Wyn's finger, and below it a shiny new gold band.

You know that dream you have when you're walking down the hall of your high school and realize that you not only forgot to prepare for a math exam but that you're stark naked? That literally can't begin to compare to the way I felt standing there, the ultimate party crasher, with everybody looking uncomfortable and uncertain and embarrassed, not because of me, but *for* me. Buck picked up a paper napkin and wiped the frosting from his face. Wyn turned away, refusing to meet my eyes. I couldn't think of a single thing to say.

I cleared my throat, tried to smile, tried to make words come out. I couldn't. So I simply turned and walked away, feeling like a perfect idiot.

CHAPTER THREE

I crossed the covered walkway between the public safety building and courthouse, my cheeks burning with the kind of humiliation that makes you want to hide in a dark room someplace and not come out for a while. I really didn't know where I was going, or care; I just wanted to get away from all of those awkward, pitying gazes.

It was stupid. It wasn't as though I had any claim on Buck, or wanted to. I was with someone else. He was with someone else. But he married her. And I hadn't known.

Buck was married.

I sat down abruptly on a curved concrete bench beneath the shade of a big oak tree, staring straight ahead at nothing at all, willing my cheeks to cool and my breathing to slow, until I suddenly realized where I was. Then it was a moment before I could breathe at all. I twisted my fingers together in my lap, hard.

Jolene sat down stiffly beside me. "I don't like you," she said, "and I don't want to be your friend.

But no woman deserves to be ambushed like that. I thought you knew, or I would've said something at the diner."

Jolene's dog Nike had found the first bomb less than twelve feet from where we were sitting. Miles and Melanie and Cisco and Pepper had been in the car right there, four easy strides away. A prickly film of perspiration broke out on my skin, and the shady air chilled it.

"It's not like she hasn't been flashing that ring around the office since before I got here," Jolene went on. Apparently she thought I'd want to know. I didn't. "I guess they got married last night at the courthouse, didn't want a fuss. Some of the staff girls found out about it and wanted to surprise them with a cake. Stupid. Unprofessional. I guess you can get away with that kind of thing in a hick town like this."

"I have nightmares sometimes," I said. I intended my voice to be conversational, but was surprised at how thin and wavery it sounded, with a little catch at the end. I knotted my fingers together even more tightly.

"Stop it," Jolene said.

But I couldn't. "The thing is," I went on rapidly, "I always wake up before the bomb goes off." My breath was coming fast, a little shakily. "I know it's going to happen and I'm trying to warn people, but nobody will listen, and when I wake up it's almost worse because I think if I could have stayed asleep a few more seconds I might could have saved them."

"Stop it," she repeated fiercely. "Don't you let that bunch of redneck fools come out and see you sitting here crying over some man."

"I'm not—"

"I know that," she said shortly, "but they don't. Take a breath, get yourself together, or I swear I'll pinch a black and blue mark on you."

That surprised a laugh out of me. "My grandmother used to say that." When I swiped a knuckle under my eye there was moisture there, but when two deputies came out of the building across the walkway and glanced in our direction I was glad they saw me sitting there laughing with Jolene.

"Everybody's grandmother used to say that." She stood, glaring at me. "I've got work to do. Don't you have someplace to be?"

I glanced at my watch. "Yep, sure do." I stood up too and added casually, "Let's have lunch some time."

I knew that would annoy her, and so it did. Her frown only deepened, and she walked away without another word. But I felt a little better as I went back to my car and drove out of town.

Crystal greeted me with a big smile from behind the desk when I walked into the vet's office. "Good news," she said. "We found her vet and they faxed over her shot records." She presented some papers to me. "She's good to go until March. Also, we got a phone number for the owner, but it goes to voice mail." Now her smile turned to a grimace. "Probably their home number, a Virginia area code. Seriously, you'd think people would learn to put their cell phones as contact numbers on the microchip. You're out of town, you lose your dog, what good does it do to have people calling your home phone to tell you they've found your dog?"

"Maybe they don't have a cell phone," I suggested, and Crystal, who was twenty-something, rolled her eyes at the very thought.

"Anyway, I left a couple of messages, your number and ours. The microchip company and the dog's vet are doing the same thing, so maybe it won't be too long before we hear something."

"Thanks," I said, glancing over the paperwork. The dog's name was Cameo, and she belonged to April Madison of 238 Willow Drive, Highlands, Virginia. "What about this?" I pointed to a line on the second page. "Greg Sellers, the emergency contact?"

"Disconnected."

I muttered, "Great. Why don't people keep their information updated?"

Crystal shrugged. "Hold on, I'll get her."

The way a dog can affect your mood is nothing short of miraculous. I still had that same hollow soreness in the pit of my stomach that I'd taken with me from the sheriff's office, but the moment Crystal came out with that fluffy white golden retriever pulling on the end of the leash, her fur combed out and shining with conditioner, her deep brown eyes bright and alert, I all but forgot my own troubles. I dropped to one knee, opening my arms as I exclaimed softly, "Look at you!"

Crystal dropped the leash a few feet away and Cameo came right to me. I gave her a big hug and ran my fingers through slightly damp, sweet smelling fur. She wagged her tail and bumped my chin with her forehead, clearly accustomed to being fawned over.

"I think she's glad to be cleaned up," said Doc, coming out behind Crystal. "She checks out fine. I couldn't find a mark on her. I don't know what she got into. A deer carcass maybe? But I doubt she ate any of it. She looks too healthy to've been eating carrion, and I don't think she could've been on the loose more than a day or two. I guess Crystal told you we got hold of her vet and have a lead on the owner, so maybe this one will be a happy ending."

"Thanks, Doc." I caught up the leash and stood. "I could use a happy ending or two right now."

He winked at me. "I'll put it on your tab."

Doc Witherspoon's office is on the edge of town, in a building next to his house, which makes it practical for late night emergencies. It's on a rural road with mostly farms nearby, and the closest house was an easy quarter-mile away. So naturally I noticed, as I made the turn out of his dirt driveway, that there was a blue sedan parked on the shoulder of the road about a hundred feet to the north. At first I thought the car was abandoned, but when I passed it I glanced in the rearview mirror and saw a man straighten up behind the wheel, as though he had been checking the glove box or reaching for something on the passenger side floor. Or trying to hide.

Because I swear, just for a moment there, the guy looked enough like that crazy tourist from town that I actually tapped my brakes to get a better look. It was too late though. He pulled off the shoulder and made a U-turn to go the opposite way, cell phone pressed to his ear. And while I didn't get a look at his face, I could tell he was straight-shouldered, not stooped, wearing a red polo shirt, not a plaid cotton one, and if he was balding, a baseball cap covered it. He was just a guy who had pulled over to the side of the road to make a phone call.

Maybe Marshall Becker was right. Maybe I *was* paranoid.

On my way home I passed the fairgrounds, where the big Ferris wheel was already being erected and the colorful tops of canvas tents were being stretched between metal poles. There were several tractor trailers and a half dozen pickup trucks parked in the dusty lot, and I could hear the staccato sound of hammers as I passed. As a kid I used to love to watch them put together the Ferris wheel, and somehow always found a way to sneak past the fence meant to keep civilians out and watch in big-eyed wonder until Uncle Ro sent a deputy to chase us off. By "us" I mean, of course, Buck and me. We were inseparable even then.

It was a quarter till three when I got home, which meant I would have to hustle if I expected to finish all the grooming clients and have them—as well as the day care dogs—ready for pickup at 5:00. And if either one of those girls even so much as mentioned leaving early today, I would strangle her.

I hurried Cameo into the rescue run and made sure she had fresh water and access to shade, as well as a chew bone I'd just sanitized in the dishwasher that morning. Then I changed my nice blouse for another faded Dog Daze tee shirt and crossed the driveway to the kennel office at a brisk pace.

The first thing I noticed was that there was a bicycle parked inside the gate. It had a duffle bag sporting a red, white, and blue design strapped to the back fender, and a helmet painted with neon color paw prints dangling from the handlebars. Odd. I didn't know anyone with a bicycle like that. Or with a bicycle of any kind, come to think of it.

There were no dogs in the play yard, and all was relatively quiet as I came up, which was always a good sign. I was starting to think a little more favorably about the girls by the time I reached my office. There I stopped dead.

The strangest-looking young man I'd ever seen was sitting behind my desk, talking on my phone. He had wild frizzy hair that was literally the color of fresh carrots, and it stuck out from his head about four inches in all directions. His eyebrows and eyelashes were also orange, although half-covered by square-framed white-rimmed glasses. He wore a bright yellow shirt with puffy short sleeves and a red bow tie. He was saying into my phone, "That's right, Mrs. Carver, ten o'clock on Thursday. We'll see you then. 'Ta!" He jotted something down on my calendar as he hung up the phone, and then leapt up from behind the desk, his smile as big as Colorado, his hands extended in joyful welcome.

"Raine Stockton!" he cried. "Raine Stockton, I can't believe it's really you!"

I just stood there, staring with mouth slightly ajar, frozen in place, and he rushed around the desk toward me. He wore the smallest pair of shorts I'd ever seen on a man, and electric blue Crocs. "I am *such* a fan!" he gushed. "I can't tell you what an honor! I've been counting the days, the hours really ..."

He was coming at me with such enthusiasm that I thought he was going to try to hug me, and I threw my hands up in self-defense. "Hey!" I said, using the same tone I'd use with an overly exuberant puppy, and he stopped like a well trained dog. I demanded, "Who are you?"

He crossed his hands over his chest in a gesture of contrition. "Where *are* my manners?" He spun on his heel and snatched a paper from my desk. "Cornelius Sylvester Lancaster the Third, at your service. I'm your twelve o'clock. My resume."

He presented the paper to me with a flourish, and I stared at it for a moment, uncomprehending. Then I had to stifle a groan. The kid I was supposed to interview at noon for the job. I'd forgotten. Still ...

"Where's Cisco?" I demanded sharply. A sudden alarm overtook me and I whirled for the door. "Where are my dogs? Where are the girls?"

I ran out into the hall and pushed open the metal fire door that led to the kennel area. "Cisco! Mischief, Magic, Pepper!"

That of course incited an immediate eruption of wild, discordant barks, but among the excited voices I thought I recognized some familiar tones from the playroom. I hurried in and found Cisco, Pepper, Mischief, and Magic safely inside the roomy "resting" kennels I used for agility lessons when dogs were awaiting their turn. I went quickly to each of them, doling out treats from my pockets and assuring myself they were all okay.

Cornelius followed me in some confusion. "Um, they were having nap time."

I whirled once again. "Where are the girls? They're supposed to be in charge."

He still looked confused. "They left at two. They said it was Thursday."

I stared at him for another moment. I knew that. Of course I did. On Thursdays the girls left at two. I had just forgotten it was Thursday.

I said, "Look, um, Cornelius ..."

"Corny," he injected. "My friends call me Corny."

I wondered if those people were really his friends, and it took me a moment to recompose thoughts. "Um, Corny, I'm sorry I missed our appointment, but this is really not a good time. I have five grooming clients to finish ..."

"Done," he said cheerfully.

I stared at him. "What?"

He held up a finger and went to the door, calling out in a singsong voice, "Ladies! Gentlemen! Please!"

To my absolute astonishment, the uproar of barking dissipated, little by little, until all that was left was the lone, determine yip of a Chihuahua at the far end of the run. Corny said sternly, "Chi-Chi!" and even that stopped. Even my own dogs settled down in their kennels and stretched out their paws, their eyes fixed upon the creature who may or may not have been the God of All Dogs.

He turned to me, smiling broadly. "Sorry. Go ahead."

I was starting to get a little spooked. "As I was saying, my grooming clients ..."

"Right." He counted them off on his fingers. "Caesar and Cicero, baths and nail trims, picked up by their moms at one thirty. They left checks, but I didn't enter them into the computer because I don't know your password. Breeze, flea-dip and blow out, went home at two. Samson is still in the drying cage. Peaches's card said she gets a puppy cut, so that's what I gave her, plus a fluff-and-buff, and her mom is on the way now."

I felt the breath go out of my chest. "You *trimmed* one of my dogs?"

"Well, I only—"

But I heard nothing else. I pushed past him rudely, racing toward the grooming room.

Peaches was a two-year-old miniature poodle and one of my best customers. Her owner brought her in every two weeks for a bath and nail trim and once a month for a full cut. And she was very particular about how that cut was done.

Peaches greeted me by coming to the front of her cage and wagging her stubby little tail as I came in. She had a peach-colored bow atop her head and peach nail polish on her nails. The cut looked perfect, but I took her out of the cage anyway and examined her for razor burn or other signs of mishandling.

"I hope I didn't overstep with the color scheme," Corny said behind me, sounding a little anxious. "It just seemed that with her name being Peaches ..."

"No." I blew out a breath of relief and gave Peaches a treat before I put her back in the cage. "No, it's fine. Everything looks fine. Only you can't just ..." I turned back to him, and then stopped as something occurred to me. "Cornelius Lancaster," I said suddenly, remembering. "There was a famous dog handler by that name. You wouldn't by any chance ..."

He nodded enthusiastically, beaming at me. "My grandfather. One hundred forty-eight best-in-shows, including three at Westminster. Two hundred sixty best of group, three hundred eighty best of breed, and heaven knows how many championships. It's kind of the family business."

"Oh," I said, staring at him. "Oh, wow. Well, that's impressive, of course, but ..."

My cell phone rang and I took it out of my pocket to check the caller ID. I held up a finger and said to Corny, "Stay here. Don't touch anything. Don't do anything. I'll be right back."

I walked quickly out of the room as I answered the call. "Miles," I said. "Hey."

"Hey, sugar." He sounded a little distracted. "It's good to hear your voice."

"Yours, too." I pushed through the metal door and walked back toward my office. "I was starting to worry."

"I'm sorry, baby. Things are a little more complicated here than I expected, and I didn't want to discuss them in front of Mel. But we need to talk."

Even under the best of circumstances, those words would make any woman pay attention. But as I reached the front of the building I heard a car door slam, and when I looked out the front windows everything inside me went still. I said, "Miles, I have to call you back."

I disconnected and walked out the front door just as Buck opened the gate. Our eyes met for a moment, and I almost thought he hesitated. Then he came through the gate, closed it behind him, and started up the walkway toward me. I stood in the blistering sun and let him.

I'd been in love with Buck Lawson since I was fifteen years old. Except for a brief time in college, I had never been with anyone else. I married him when I was twenty-two years old, divorced him when I found out he was cheating on me, and married him again a year later. That marriage wasn't much better than the first, and we spent almost as much of it apart as we did together. I divorced him for the last time in October of the previous year, when I found him in bed with Wyn, who was his coworker and, at that time, my friend.

It sounds like a soap opera and it doesn't show either one of us in a very good light, but the truth is that things have always been more complex between us than they seem. It's hard to just walk away from someone you've been with half your life. Hard for me, hard for him. We'd grown up together, we went to church together, we'd had Christmas and Thanksgiving and Fourth of July barbecues together for as long as I could remember. He was the one who'd given me Cisco, and to this day I think Cisco considers himself as much Buck's dog as mine. How do you erase a history like that? How do you just stop being who you've always been?

He stood in front of me, close enough for me to smell the baked cotton of his uniform shirt, the faint familiar trace of his sweat. His eyes were squinted in the sun as he looked at me, and for a moment he didn't say anything. Then, "You know I didn't want that to happen."

I said nothing.

"I've been trying to tell you for weeks," he said. "All summer, I guess. Neither one of us wanted you to be blindsided. But that's exactly what happened. I'm sorry."

The ache in my stomach was back again, but I was very proud of how calm my voice was as I said, "What do you expect from me, Buck?"

"Nothing." He was quick enough to admit that. Good for him. "I just wanted you to know I didn't mean to hurt you."

"You never do." I regretted that the minute I said it, because the last thing I wanted was to let him think he'd hurt me at all. I added irritably, "Is that it? Because I'm busy."

I started to turn away, but he said, "No. No, there's something else."

I looked back at him impatiently.

I saw him swallow. He shifted his gaze briefly over my shoulder, and then back again. He said, "I don't want you to hear it from somebody else. There's a baby, Raine. Wyn is pregnant."

A few months ago, I fell hard at an agility trial, literally knocking the breath out of myself. I remember that awful few seconds of floundering like a fish on the dock, wheezing and gasping with lungs that wouldn't expand, until suddenly air came rushing in again. This was like that. Only it seemed like much longer than a few seconds before I could breathe again this time.

Finally I said, "Wow." My lips felt heavy and my voice sounded odd and lifeless, even to my own ears. Still, I managed, "Congratulations. I know that's what you've always wanted."

I turned to go back inside, but before I had even completed the first step I spun around, palm out, and struck him hard across the face. "You *coward!*"

I stood there with fists clenched and eyes blazing, fighting the urge to hit him again. "That was for Wyn," I said, breathing hard.

The force of my blow had left a welt across his cheek that was sure to bruise, and every time someone asked him about it he would remember this moment. I wanted to take satisfaction in that, but I couldn't. Because when I looked into his eyes I did not see anger, or embarrassment, or even surprise. What I saw was relief. He had done something wrong, and now he had been punished. He thought it was over.

And he was right. It was.

Suddenly I was very tired. "Get out of here, Buck," I said.

I turned to walk back to my office, and this time I didn't look back.

CHAPTER FOUR

I walked back into my office and sat down behind the desk. I drew in one long breath and blew it out through my lips. I moved the papers around on my desk. I leaned back in my chair and stared sightlessly at the SPCA poster of a puppy behind bars on the opposite wall.

Corny tiptoed in with his hands wrapped around one of my Dog Daze mugs. From the size of his eyes behind those absurd glasses, I guessed he had witnessed my assault on a police officer and was wondering whether he had just applied for a job with someone who was about to go to jail. He set the cup carefully on the desk before me.

"It's chamomile," he said, almost whispering. "I found it in the kitchenette. I hope you don't mind. Very soothing."

I stared at him.

"Well," he murmured, taking a few steps backwards. "I guess I'll just, um …" He gestured vaguely toward the door.

I blinked and managed to focus. I cleared my throat. "Thank you for the tea, Corny," I said. "That was nice." I took a sip and he regarded me with slightly less wariness. "And thanks for your help with the dogs while I was gone. I appreciate your enthusiasm."

He smiled cautiously. "I love dogs. And they seem to like me."

I took another sip of tea. "What did you mean, before, when you said you were my biggest fan?"

His eyes lit up and he pressed his hands together with excitement as he came back to my desk. "Well," he confessed, "I've followed you on Facebook for, like, *ever*, and there was that great piece you did in *Clean Run* on proof-training contact points, and then year before last? When Cisco found that little girl who was lost in the woods and kept her warm all night?" He drew in a dramatic breath and clasped his hands over his heart. "Everyone in the whole *state* thought she was dead! Then of course there was that awful business with the New Day Wilderness Retreat, and how you and Cisco helped all those kids survive in a *blizzard*! I mean, the work you do! And then *Dog Fancy* did that feature on Camp Bowser-Wowser a couple of years back and I thought what you said about teaching scent-training was just brilliant."

He must have seen me tense because a shadow of compassion came over his eyes as he added, "And then of course with all the publicity about what happened there last month, well …" The shadow was gone and the excitement was back. "You and Cisco are practically national heroes! How could I *not* be a fan? And when I saw on your website that you were looking for help ..."

He rushed forward and sank into the chair that was pushed up against the wall near my desk, his hands clasped before him in supplication. "Oh, Miss Stockton! Working for you would be a dream come true!"

Over the top? Without a doubt. Unbelievable—as in seriously, unbelievable? You bet. But as I sat there considering the way my day had been going so far, Cornelius Lancaster the Third was the least bizarre thing that had happened to me.

I glanced down at his resume. "You're from Chapel Hill?"

He nodded happily. "Very near."

"Degree in Animal Behavioral Science from Duke?" I raised an eyebrow, impressed.

"Working on it," he assured me.

I said, "Look, Corny, I really can't afford to pay that much ..."

"Don't worry about it." He gave a blithe wave of his hand. "I have a trust fund."

I stared at him for another moment, then glanced back down at the resume. The usual pet store jobs, references from professors and past employers ... but a trust fund kid? Really?

He said quickly, "I've been grooming dogs since I was eight years old. I can clip to standard any breed in the AKC. I won my first championship with a King Charles Cavalier when I was twelve and I've been showing dogs ever since. I also took two semesters of business and I majored in computer science for about six months, so I can be a real asset to you in the office. I don't mind cleaning kennels. It would be an *honor* to clean kennels for you. I can—"

"I know, you're very qualified, and I'm sure you'd do a good job," I was compelled to interrupt. "It's just that—"

"Miss Stockton," he said earnestly, pressing his hands together between his knees. "My dream is to open a rehabilitation facility for abused and neglected dogs and train them to perform specialized tasks for disabled servicemen. If I could apprentice under you, get hands-on training in a genuine operating facility like Dog Daze, that would put me light years closer to what I was put on this earth to do. Let me prove myself to you. Give me a chance."

I looked at him for another moment. Even I couldn't believe the words that came out of my mouth next. "All right," I said. "We'll give it a shot. Twelve dollars an hour for the first two weeks and if it works out, fifteen dollars an hour after that. Ten to three six days a week."

His face lit up like Christmas morning. "Do you mean it? I have the job?"

"Well, there's paperwork. I have to check your references, I need you to fill out a W-4 ..."

"Thank you!' He jumped to his feet and grabbed my hand, pumping it enthusiastically. "Thank you! You won't regret it, I swear! I won't let you down!"

Taking everything into consideration, there was no way he could.

With Corny's bouncing-ball energy and hamster-like speed, the kennels were cleaned, the boarders were exercised, and the day care clients were brushed, treated, and ready to go home by four thirty. Mrs. Sullivan loved Peaches's puppy cut and gushed over the peach nail polish. She tipped ten dollars and I gave it to Corny. He protested, but I am always fair with my employees. He volunteered to stay until all the kennel dogs were fed and tucked away for the night, but I sent him home as soon as the last day care dog was picked up. He strapped on his paw print helmet and pedaled off happily on his bicycle, promising to be back bright and early the next morning.

I was thinking how a helmet like that would make a nice birthday present for Melanie when I realized I had forgotten to call Miles back. I promised myself I'd do it as soon as I closed up the kennel for the day, but I think I knew even then I wouldn't. I just didn't have the strength to deal with one more man today.

At five o'clock I let Mischief, Magic, Pepper, and Cisco out for one last romp, then took them up to the house to introduce them to the new dog. The best way to introduce two unfamiliar dogs is on leash, one at a time, and in neutral territory. Cisco and the Aussies are so accustomed to meeting strange dogs that they are practically disinterested, but I wasn't so sure about Pepper. She was not even a year old and still full of puppy golden retriever exuberance, so I took her out to meet Cameo first while the other dogs waited in the house.

I had no sooner opened the gate to the rescue run than I heard the *clack* of claws against the kitchen window, and I glanced over my shoulder to see Cisco standing on his back legs, scratching at the window and grinning at us. As soon as Cameo trotted into view, he started barking and clawing at the window again; clearly, he felt he was entitled by virtue of rank to be the first to meet the new dog. Of course, once Pepper heard her idol bark she lost all but the most cursory interest in Cameo and started lunging happily toward Cisco. We had to have a few obedience reminders before I took Pepper back inside. Mischief was next, then Magic. After the routine sniffing and circling, Cameo seemed to dismiss the Aussies as beneath her regal notice, and my girls, as I'd expected, were far more interested in exploring the smells of the rescue run, where they rarely got to visit, than in yet another golden retriever.

Cisco was an entirely different story.

I put the other dogs inside while I prepared what I intended to be a brief on-leash introduction, but I had barely opened the door to escort Mischief inside when Cisco, his patience apparently at an end, dashed past me and out into the yard. Cisco's door manners are not entirely flawless, but he definitely knows better than that, and I'll admit he took me by surprise. I cried, "Cisco!" and spun around to chase him, but I needn't have worried. He ran straight to the rescue run and flung his paws up on the gate, his tongue lolling with excitement as he tossed a glance over his shoulder at me. I unclipped Mischief's leash and closed the door firmly behind me as I hurried to Cisco.

By the time I got there, the two goldens were sniffing each other through the chain link. I snapped the leash onto Cisco's collar before allowing him inside. Cisco's exuberance can be a little overwhelming under the best of circumstances, and I didn't want him trying her patience. But the minute I opened the gate Cisco practically dragged me through it, and a series of blur spins and play bows convinced me the safest thing I could do for all concerned was to let Cisco off his leash and allow the two dogs to romp.

I laughed out loud as Cisco ran up to Cameo, bumped her shoulder, and took off in the opposite direction. She gave chase, and it was good to see her run like a normal, happy dog. Cisco found a stick and they played tug for a while. Cisco won the game of tug and ran away with the stick. Cameo pretended disinterest until Cisco circled back around and dropped the stick at her feet. In a flash, Cameo snatched it up and took off around the fence perimeter with Cisco in hot pursuit. I swear, the sheer innocent delight of dogs at play can heal the rawest wound, and I could have stood there all day watching them.

But once again I heard the clack of claws at the kitchen window and when I looked around it was Pepper, scratching on the glass and emitting her high-pitched puppy bark. She hated to be left out, and it was time for her dinner. I called Cisco to me and both dogs galloped up, pink tongues waving happily. I ruffled their fur and tugged their ears.

"I'm glad you made a friend," I told Cameo. And I added to Cisco as I snapped on his leash, "But don't you get too attached. She's got a home. She's only visiting."

Feeding five dogs in one kitchen is a bit much, even for me, especially when two of those dogs are new to the pack. So I prepared Cameo's dinner and took it to her in the rescue run, then put Pepper in her crate with her own bowl—a bright red ceramic one, I might add, embossed in silver with Pepper's name and silver paw prints that Melanie had custom-ordered from a jewelry store in New York. She does tend to spoil that puppy, and her dad isn't much better.

My three dogs waited in a patient, expectant sit while I doled out their meals into plain old stainless steel bowls. I was just putting the last bowl on the floor when my landline rang. I released the dogs with a hand signal and watched them dive into their meals as I answered it. It was my Aunt Mart.

"Hey, Raine," she said. "Ro and I were just sitting here talking about throwing some chicken kebabs on the grill and we wondered if you wouldn't like to come over for supper. I'm making apple slaw and a nice key lime pie for dessert. You know, that heart-healthy diet the doctors have got your uncle on isn't half bad once you get used to it. And I've already lost ten pounds! Of course, that's without the pie."

I knew, of course, that she had not called just to invite me to supper. And as tempting as the menu sounded, I really wasn't up to spending an evening with my aunt and uncle tiptoeing around Buck's big news. I said, as cheerily as I could manage, "Thanks, Aunt Mart, it sounds great! But I just put a casserole in the oven." The casserole in question was not exactly in my oven and would probably come in a cardboard box proclaiming it to be the healthiest frozen dinner on the market. And the sad thing was, it probably also would be the healthiest thing in my freezer, if not the only thing.

"Oh, honey, a casserole in this heat? How can you stand it?"

"Besides, I've really got my hands full here," I went on. "You know how crazy it gets this time of year, and I just took in a new rescue dog. Say ..." I plunged right into the subject to save her the awkwardness of trying to figure out how to bring it up herself. "Did you hear about Buck and Wyn?"

"Yes, I did." There was a slight hesitance in her voice, but also a hint of relief. "That was awfully sudden, don't you think?"

"Oh, I don't know." It was something of a struggle to keep my tone casual, and I hoped Aunt Mart didn't notice. "I think they've been planning it for a while."

"I suppose." She sounded concerned, which meant I probably wasn't doing as good a job about disguising my feelings as I'd hoped. "I just don't understand why he didn't tell anybody. I feel sorry for the girl, in a way, not having a proper ceremony and all."

I felt sorry for her too, but not for that reason. "Well, I guess they didn't want a fuss."

She sighed. "I hate change. He's been part of the family for so long. It's going to feel strange thinking about him with someone else."

I soldiered on. "Well, the more things change ..."

I lost my thought and trailed off, and her silence was sympathetic. "Raine, honey …"

I said quickly, "Look, Aunt Mart, I've got to run. Five dogs in the house and all that."

"Well, you take care of yourself in this heat. Lord, I don't know what we're going to do if we don't get some rain. My garden's as dry as a bone yard. I picked you a basket of tomatoes this morning but they go bad awfully fast this time of year, so if you don't get over here in the next day or two, I'll have Ro leave them on your porch."

"Thanks, Aunt Mart," I said, although the last thing I wanted to see was another tomato. That was something else everyone was tired of by now—which was why everybody I knew kept bringing their tomatoes to me. "I'll try to run by some time tomorrow."

"Don't you work too hard, you hear?"

"Yes, ma'am. And Aunt Mart?" I added just before I hung up. "Save me a piece of that pie, will you?"

She chuckled and promised she would, and I hoped she was a little less worried about me than she had been when she'd first called.

The next phone call was from Sonny, and it came just as I was putting away the dog dishes. I had already let the house dogs out into the exercise yard and was thinking about allowing Cameo to join them when the phone rang.

"Hi, Raine," Sonny said. "I just thought I'd call and check on—"

"I'm fine, I'm fine," I interrupted. My frustration at having had to be so polite about the whole thing with my aunt came out sounding like impatience as I went on, "I'm not the one people should be worried about. Wyn is. You know the only reason he married her is because of the election, and that's just creepy. I mean, they've been living together right under everybody's noses, not to mention working together, all summer, and you heard she's pregnant, right? How's that going to look on election day? Of course they had to hurry up and get married before the newspaper picked a candidate, or she started showing, whichever came first. The whole thing is just so sneaky. So *political*."

There was a brief silence, and then Sonny said, "Actually, I just called to check on the dog Rick brought in this morning. But, oh my. It sounds like you've had an interesting day."

I crinkled up my face in a grimace that barely reflected my mortification, and I was glad she couldn't see. I had no choice then but to tell her the whole sordid story, beginning with how I'd unwittingly walked in on a wedding reception to which I had not been invited, and ending with how I'd tried to punch Buck out on my front walk. "I don't know if they're telling anybody about the baby yet," I added, somewhat reluctantly. "So you probably shouldn't spread it around." Although why I was protecting them I didn't know.

Sonny said thoughtfully, "I haven't known either you or Buck all that long, but this seems so bizarre to me. I could have sworn he was still carrying a torch for you."

I didn't like to say so, but there had been more than one incident over the past few months that made me think the same thing. Perhaps what I was really upset about was that I had allowed myself to be so misled.

"Of course," Sonny went on, "you divorced him for a reason, remember? I do like Buck, but he was not a good husband to you and, even though this must be painful—endings always are—maybe you could look at it as a good thing."

"I do," I assured her quickly, albeit in a voice that was still tense with the bitter taste of emotions I'd sooner forget. "I'm relieved, really. I'm glad he's moved on. It's just the way he did it was so …"

"Cowardly," she supplied for me, and I sighed.

"Exactly."

She sighed too. "Men," she said. "They live by their own rules, don't they?"

I took the phone out onto the back porch and sat down on the steps so that I could watch the dogs. Cisco ran the length of the exercise yard closest to the rescue pen, occasionally emitting a bark that would cause Cameo to look up from munching grass. Pepper chased him, nipping at his tail feathers, and he ignored her. He had eyes for no dog but Cameo. Mischief and Magic were always happiest in each others' company, and took turns playing tag-team relay with a dog-proof soccer ball with a handle on it.

"Anyway," I added, "I didn't mean to go off like that. Thanks for calling about the dog. It turns out she was perfectly healthy, with a microchip, and we've got phone numbers. So maybe it won't be too long before we find her folks."

"Didn't you say there was blood on her coat?"

"Doc couldn't figure out where it came from any more than I could. Sometimes if a dog has been on the run for a while it'll be hungry enough to eat a squirrel or a rabbit, or she might have come across something already dead." But even as I said it I was uneasy. Those explanations had never sounded right to me, and they were no more convincing now.

"Raine ..." Sonny's voice sounded thoughtful, maybe even worried. "Something happened to that dog. I haven't been able to put my finger on it, but she was awfully stressed out this morning."

"Well," I admitted, "any lost dog is going to be stressed. Especially a pampered house pet lost in the woods. She had one of those designer collars with rhinestones on it, definitely not a dog used to roughing it."

"No, it was more than that," Sonny insisted. "She was traumatized. She had been through something, was worried about something. She felt guilty."

"Oh," I said, trying not to roll my eyes. "Your superpower."

Although an otherwise rational person, Sonny occasionally got "impressions" from animals that even less rational people might call communication. I myself am extremely rational, and while I absolutely believe in talking to dogs, I have a problem when the dogs start talking back.

"Raine." There was mild admonishment in her tone. "You have to admit I'm right more often than not."

She had me there. I refuse to call her a pet psychic, but the things she had purportedly learned from dogs had proven to be unerringly accurate, if often hard to interpret. So even though I pretended to be skeptical, I always listened.

"Okay, I'll bite," I said. "What was she guilty about?"

"I'm not sure," Sonny answered. "You know how dogs are. They so often feel responsible for things that have nothing to do with them."

"Well, she seems fine now," I said, watching as Cameo came over to the fence and made eye contact with Cisco, wagging her tail. Cisco immediately spun with excitement and flung his paws up on the fence. I suppressed a chuckle. "Cisco is wild about her. They played like old pals in the rescue run this afternoon."

"Oh, that's good," Sonny said. "The poor thing needs a friend now."

"By the way," I said, "I took your advice and hired an assistant today."

"My goodness, you have had a busy day! Good for you. Who is it?"

"No one you know. Just some stalker from the Internet. He'll probably turn out to be a serial killer. He's great with the dogs, though."

She chuckled. "Well, as long as you've got some help."

Pepper, who had been trying so valiantly to get Cisco's attention all this time, gave it her best shot with a running dive and a nip on his shoulder. Cisco returned an annoyed snap and her ears went down; she tucked her tail and ran to the other side of the yard. Cisco leapt up on the fence again and barked at Cameo. I didn't want anyone's feelings to get hurt, so I decided a little judicious intervention was in order.

"I've got to go, Sonny," I said, standing. "Cisco is making an absolute fool of himself over Cameo. I've never seen him act like this before."

She laughed. "He's in love."

I started down the steps. "If they weren't both neutered, I'd be worried."

"Love is about more than sex, Raine," she advised sagely.

Once again I sighed. "Don't I know it," I said. "I'll talk to you later, Sonny."

My last duty of the day was to feed all the boarders and turn them out into their individual outdoor runs while I washed their dishes and made sure their kennels were clean and sanitized for the night. All the kennels at Dog Daze have raised beds, but some of the boarders bring their own fluffy beds, blankets, or personal toys, which sometimes become the victims of accidents during the day. I tossed a few such misfortunes into the on-site laundry and went back to my office to close out the computer.

I spent a fortune remodeling Dog Daze last year, and Miles, whose crew was in charge of construction, might have added a few items for which I was never billed—like the oversized industrial dishwasher that washed and sanitized all the dog dishes so they did not have to be done by hand—although I was never able to precisely nail him on it. The result was that Dog Daze is way more luxurious than my house, with air-conditioning and radiant heated floors throughout, piped in music, the aforementioned washer-drier, a kitchenette, two bathrooms—one with a shower so that I don't have to run back to the house to clean up when a dog throws up on me or I slip in the mud during an agility class—and even a bunk room where I'd spent more than one night during the winter simply because it was warmer than my house. So I don't really mind working long hours at Dog Daze, especially when I can take Cisco down with me and squeeze in a few extra minutes of agility practice between chores. Tonight, however, Cisco was interested in nothing but Cameo, who was still in the rescue run, and it was clear his heart was not in the practice. I left him flat on his belly with his nose pressed against the crack at the bottom of the door while I wound up the day's business.

According to the paperwork Crystal had given me on Cameo, her owner's name was April Madison of Highlands, Virginia. I knew she would have half a dozen messages already from the microchip company and from Crystal, but I wanted to make sure my contact information was also on her list, so I called and left another message. While I did so, I took Cameo's pink rhinestone collar back to the grooming room and started scrubbing out the scuffs and dirt with saddle soap. That was when I noticed something odd.

A few stitches had been neatly sliced away from the double layer of leather just near the buckle, and I could clearly see the shape of a small round object inside. I finished leaving the message for April Madison and went back to my desk where, after a moment's rummaging, I found a letter opener with which I used to pry the object out.

"Whoa, Cameo," I murmured, setting the small metal button in the center of a sheet of plain paper on my desk. "You must be more valuable than I thought."

Although I had only seen them in specialty high-tech catalogues and online, I was pretty sure what this was. It was a GPS locator of the kind commonly used by cops and spies and, more recently—and much less commonly—by owners of championship dogs and cats who had a tendency to wander. The only thing I couldn't understand is why someone who would go to all the trouble to microchip a dog *and* put a GPS locator in her collar would be careless enough to lose her in the first place.

Tourists. I'd never understand them.

CHAPTER FIVE

I live in a big old farmhouse that was built in a time before climate change, when thick green forests and a complete lack of asphalt made air-conditioning unnecessary. Even now, I make do with ceiling fans and open windows in most rooms of the house, but I relented a few years back and put a window air-conditioning unit in my upstairs bedroom, where the temperature can easily climb above eighty degrees in the daytime. The hum and hiss of its motor is soothing white noise to me, and that's probably why I did not hear the intruder until it was too late.

In fact, there's a good chance I wouldn't have heard anything at all if it hadn't been for the nightmare. The bomb, the car, Cisco, Melanie and Miles who wouldn't run no matter how much I screamed at them, no matter how hard I tried to warn them. And then a sudden, explosive sound that propelled me upright in bed with a choked, indrawn scream, my pounding heart shaking my whole body, gasping for breath. Cisco and Cameo were standing at the window that didn't contain the air-conditioning unit, heads forwards, tails curled, staring out intently. I realized that the sound that had awakened me was the bark of a dog only because, at that moment, Cameo barked again.

Of course Cameo should have been safely in her crate downstairs with Pepper, Mischief, and Magic—my bedroom really wasn't big enough for all five dogs—but the way Cisco flopped down in front of my closed door with his nose pointed downstairs, emitting a loud sigh every thirty seconds or so, assured me that the only way I'd get any sleep that night was if Cameo joined us. I brought her upstairs, Cisco forfeited his duck-printed dog bed for her, and we were all sleeping soundly by ten thirty.

And so we remained until—I squinted my eyes at the digital numbers on the clock—four forty-five. It should have been pitch dark outside, but a glow of light illuminated the two dogs at the window clearly, and above the hum of the air-conditioning I could hear the faint staccato rapid-fire barking of multiple dogs. The kennel. Something had disturbed the dogs in the kennel, and triggered the security lights.

I came to this conclusion about half a second before Cisco gave a deep determined bark, and Cameo joined in the fray. Both goldens stood with their tails curled high and their feet planted stiffly, barking at something in the yard. I rolled out of bed and rushed to the window just in time to see the shadow of a man running across my yard away from the kennel.

"Hey!" I shouted.

I flung open the door and ran down the stairs in my bare feet, followed closely by two barking, galloping golden retrievers. By this time all three dogs in the living room were awake and barking in their crates and over the cacophony. I thought I heard the sound of an engine starting. I flung open the door just in time to see the flash of taillights midway down my drive. I wouldn't have seen anything else of use at all except that the curve of my driveway brought the fleeing automobile into the momentary reflection of the kennel security lights.

It was a blue sedan.

I found my rain boots in the hall closet and pulled them on before racing across the yard in my nightshirt to the kennel building. I was vaguely aware of Cisco bounding along beside me, barking just as though the burglar—or whatever he was—had not already escaped. The window glass was unbroken, and the lock clicked open as I punched in the code on the keypad. Nonetheless I checked the petty cash and the locked drawer in my office where I kept the checks from day's receipts. All accounted for. Apparently the barking of the dogs, along with the security lights, had scared the prowler off before he was able to do any damage. What kind of idiot tries to break into a dog kennel, anyway?

One thing was certain. I was *not* calling the sheriff.

I spent fifteen minutes or so passing out treats and trying to calm down the kennel dogs, then I turned off the interior lights and used a flashlight to cross the yard back to the house. At the bottom of the steps I stopped, my heart lurching with alarm. The front door was standing wide open.

I knew exactly what had happened. I'd rushed outside, pulling the door closed behind me, only it hadn't caught. Cisco had followed me, because the instinct to run by my side was even stronger than his obsession with his new girlfriend. Cameo had no such instinct.

I caught Cisco's collar and ushered him quickly up the steps and into the house, closing the door firmly behind us. Almost as soon as I did, I could have sworn I heard the back door slam closed, and I my heart jumped to my throat. I glanced wildly around the room, closing my fingers around Cisco's fur and pulling him close. Had someone been in the house? Was he here now? What had I been thinking? I'd just seen someone running from the kennel; his partner could be inside, waiting for me; it might all have been a diversion just to get me trapped inside, and I'd been so worried about losing the dog that I'd blundered right into it. And me, a cop's wife.

Ex-wife.

I stood frozen in place for a moment, heart pounding as I strained to listen. I heard nothing except Mischief's claws clicking on the bars of her crate as she stretched to try to see what was happening. I eased open the door of the coat closet and found a heavy stick that I used to prop open the screen door when carrying things inside and, so armed, made my way through the house toward the kitchen. Cisco was fascinated by the stick and trotted beside me with his head up, waiting for me to throw it. I hoped I didn't have to.

The back door was closed, just as I had left it, and when I checked the windows everything seemed quiet. The security lights were still on and I could have easily seen someone trying to flee across the yard. And why weren't the dogs barking? If anyone had been inside my house they'd be having a fit by now. I was starting to think I'd imagined hearing the door slam when I checked the lock. The dead bolt was unlocked. I was sure I had locked it. I always lock it. Well, almost. But I'd locked it tonight ... hadn't I?

I twisted it closed and went quickly to check the rest of the house. I looked in closets and under furniture, behind draperies and in hidden cubbies. There was no sign of an intruder. And with every passing moment my heart sank deeper in my chest. Because there was also no sign of Cameo.

I called for her, I checked every room again, knowing all the while it was futile. She was a stray, she'd been frightened in the middle of the night, and there was an open door. Of course she'd bolted.

And I was as irresponsible as the owners who had lost her in the first place.

I pulled on jeans, took my flashlight, and searched the perimeter of the house, the yard, the kennel area, calling for her all the while. It's an exercise in frustration to try to find a runaway dog in the dark; believe me, I've tried it before. She could have been hiding in a dozen different places, or deliberately running from me, or, as every instinct in my body told me she had done, she could have taken off for the woods the minute she was free.

Eventually I was forced to admit defeat. I returned to the house a little before dawn, where Cisco was watching for me with his paws on the window. He looked at me anxiously when I came in and I felt just awful. I sank to the floor and put an arm around him. "Oh, Cisco," I said. "I'm so sorry."

I don't think he understood.

CHAPTER SIX

As soon as it was light, I put Cisco's tracking harness on him and took him out to search. He picked up her trail immediately, as I'd known he would, and it led straight into the woods and across the mountain, as I'd known it would. Those woods eventually join up with the Nantahala National Forest, and the odds against finding a single lost dog in all that wilderness, even with the aid of Cisco's nose, were not good.

We searched for over an hour before I reluctantly called Cisco off. He looked uncertain and confused, because he was trained to keep searching until he lost the scent, and even training exercises ended with a mock "find" and a reward. But it was after eight and I hadn't yet opened the kennel. We might well track miles into the woods on the trail of a dog who had too much of a head start to be found, and I simply couldn't afford the wasted effort. There had to be a better way.

I played a quick game of tug with Cisco and let him munch down a handful of treats before we turned back. "It's okay, boy," I told him, ruffling his ears. "We're not giving up. Just falling back to regroup."

I had given Pepper, Mischief, and Magic their breakfasts before I left, but after last night's incident I wasn't comfortable about leaving them outside while I was away, either in my double-fenced kennel play yard or my fenced backyard. So, even though the kennel dogs were waiting to begin their day with breakfast and exercise time, the first thing I did was hurry to the house to release my own three charges from their crates. Then, with Cisco beside me, I trotted across the drive to Dog Daze.

I hesitated, glancing around, when I saw the bicycle with the paw print helmet dangling from the handlebars parked outside the gate. But when I heard the barking of a couple of dogs in their outside kennel runs, I hurried up the walk. The door was unlocked and I rushed inside. "Corny?"

He called cheerfully back, "Good morning, Miss Stockton!" He came from the kitchenette with a mug of steaming black coffee, which he presented to me. Cisco raced to greet him and sat, without being asked, at his feet, grinning up at him. Corny stroked Cisco's ears and added, "The dogs are fed, the dishes are in the dishwasher, Chi-Chi and Dimples have had their meds, and I've just started opening the kennel runs. Oh, and I stopped by a farm stand on the way in for fresh blueberry muffins. I left one on your desk, warm from the micro."

I stared at him. He was dressed today in red plaid Bermuda shorts and an emerald green shirt with white piping around the collar, matching green Crocs, and white socks. But that was not why I stared. "How did you get in here?" I demanded.

He straightened up from petting Cisco and looked confused. "The door?"

"It was locked."

"Oh." He waved that away. "I used the code."

I glared at him suspiciously. "I didn't give you the code."

"Well, it was easy enough to figure out." He looked pleased with himself. "Cisco's birthday."

Now I was the one who was confused. "How do you know Cisco's birthday?"

He widened his eyes in every appearance of sincerity. "Doesn't everyone?"

I sucked in a breath, and let it go. Two things were clear: I had to get a better security system, and I had to stop being so suspicious. The man had brought me coffee, for heaven's sakes. *And* fresh blueberry muffins. And he'd fed the dogs and washed the dishes and Cisco adored him. So I said, in a much more patient tone than I had originally intended, "Listen, you really can't just …"

And then I stopped as something occurred to me. "Corny, you didn't happen to come back here last night, did you?" So much for not being so suspicious. "Maybe for something you forgot?"

"Gracious, no." He smiled confidently. "I hardly ever forget things. Organization is the key to a happy life."

I nodded, making such an effort to keep my expression pleasant and nonjudgmental that it's a wonder my skin didn't crack. I pretended to turn toward my office, and then looked back. "Oh, by the way ... what kind of car do you drive? I need to know for, you know, the employment papers."

The minute I said it I felt like a jerk. He made coffee. He brought muffins. He had *not* been tailing me in a dark blue sedan and he had not tried to break into the kennel last night. Why should he have, when he obviously could have just used the keypad? I was not just a jerk, but a stupid one as well.

But Corny looked not in the least offended. "Oh, I don't have a car," he assured me breezily. "They wreak absolute havoc on the environment. I'm a cycler all the way."

"But ..." Again I stared at him, somewhat at a loss for words. A bicycle might work fine on a college campus or in a suburban area like Chapel Hill, but these were the mountains, for heaven's sake, with nothing but long rural highways to connect the widely scattered farms and houses to town. I finished lamely, "Are you staying nearby?"

"Not far," he replied cheerfully.

I should have been more persistent, but I already felt bad about practically accusing him of attempted B&E, and after he had come in early to feed the dogs. Besides, the faint sugary aroma of warm blueberry muffins lingered in the air, beckoning me toward my office. "Well," I said, turning that way, "stop by my office when you get a chance and fill out the employment application and W-4. I'll leave them on my desk. Go ahead and let the rest of the dogs out. I've got some phone calls to make."

"Sure thing, Miss Stockton." He practically skipped through the metal doors and down the corridor toward the kennels. I had to admit, I had never had an employee this excited about his job, and I resolved to be more gracious in the future.

I munched on the muffin and sipped my coffee while working up the courage to make the series of unhappy, embarrassing phone calls that were awaiting. The first one was to the vet's office, just so they wouldn't be surprised should someone happen to bring in the lost dog they had last released to my care. I admit, I was half hoping someone already had, but no such luck. The second was to the ranger station, where I left a message for Rick. I left a message on the machine of our newly opened animal shelter, just in case someone spotted her on the road and had the good sense to take her to the shelter. Then I started calling my neighbors up and down the highway, asking them to please call me with any sign of the missing golden retriever—not that they would have done otherwise. When it comes to dogs, I am everyone's first phone call around here.

All the while, Cisco lay patiently beside my desk gazing up at me in hopes of a dropped muffin crumb. Because I felt so bad about losing his girlfriend in the first place, I saved the last bite for him—even though, to be honest, it was so good I wanted it all. While he licked his lips, I picked up Corny's resume and dialed the first number on his list of references. It was a pet store whose doors had long since closed, telephone disconnected. The second was a grooming salon that didn't keep records back that far. The third one claimed to remember Corny fondly, although they kept referring to him as a her and calling him "Corkie," and gave him—or her—the highest recommendation. Coming from an assistant manager who didn't sound old enough to be giving one anyone a recommendation, I supposed it was a start. The last call I made was to a Professor Rudolph; it went to voice mail so I left a message.

All the time I was on the phone, I absently turned Cameo's pink collar around and around between my fingers. I had left it on my desk to dry after scrubbing it, so now she was out in the wilderness without even a collar. Not that it would have made a difference, with no tags, and even the little tracking button I'd found removed. But what was I supposed to do? I had a full kennel for the weekend, more day care dogs coming in, and a half day's worth of grooming to do. I couldn't just take off into the woods looking for a dog who wasn't even mine.

Cisco tilted his head toward me in a way that looked remarkably like a reproach.

I heard Marilee come in, followed in a few minutes by Katie, and I went out to introduce the girls to Corny. They wrinkled up their noses when I sent them off to clean the kennels, but Corny intervened. "Already done," he told me brightly. "It doesn't take long if you have a system."

I was impressed. If he could do twice the work of the two girls in half the time, already he was saving me money. I told the girls, "Okay, go sweep the dog hair out of the playroom, and fill the swimming pools outside. Then you can start taking the boarders out to play two at a time."

They hurried off, glad to be out of kennel-sanitizing duty, and I heard the first of our day care clients pull up. It had been Melanie's idea to leave flyers advertising doggie day care in all the pet-friendly hotels, campgrounds, and cabins in this and surrounding counties, which resulted in almost more business than I could handle. I'd actually considered closing down the day care, despite the boost in income, because even with the help of the high school girls it was too much to keep up with. However, if Corny continued to prove as efficient as he had so far, this would be my most profitable summer ever.

I spent the next hour or so showing Corny how to check in our day care and grooming clients, although the truth of the matter was that he probably could have shown me, and his gushy bedside manner was so over the top that even the clingiest dog went happily with him to the playroom, and moms and dads left with carefree grins on their faces. I am always pleasant to my clients, of course, but I tend to be a little less demonstrative with my admiration than Corny was. Judging from the way the clients—not to mention the dogs—responded to him, however, I wondered if I should reconsider my approach.

I sent Corny off to bathe Petals the bull dog and started out to the play yard to set up the agility course for tomorrow morning's lesson. I was stopped by Cisco, who lay with his nose pressed so pathetically against the crack at the bottom of the door that I didn't have to be a pet psychic to know what he was thinking. How could I really go about my day as though nothing had happened when I knew there was a lost golden retriever out there somewhere? How could I give up before I tried everything in my power to find her?

I went into the grooming room, where Corny was just lifting Petals into one of the drying cages and crooning to her about how pretty she was. A beagle and a cocker spaniel waited their turns, munching on chew strips, and soothing classical music came from the radio in the corner. The entire room smelled like lavender, with barely a hint of wet dog. Usually the grooming room was a madhouse of barking dogs and blow-driers, flying fur and soap suds. Grooming was not my favorite thing and my technique probably showed it. But today the place reminded me more of an upscale beauty salon than the barely controlled chaos to which I was accustomed.

I waited until Corny latched the cage and turned the drier on low to clear my throat. "Um, Corny—"

He turned expectantly.

"I hate to leave you alone on your first day," I began, "but I lost a dog last night and ..."

His eyes flew wide and he clapped a hand over his heart. "Oh, no! Oh, who was it? No, don't tell me, I can't bear it. You must be heartbroken! How could you even come to work today? Please, let me—"

"No, no." I held up both hands to protect myself from the flood of his compassion as I said quickly, "Not lost as in dead. Just lost. I took in a rescue yesterday and she got out of the house in the middle of the night ..."

"She ran away?" If possible, he looked even more distressed.

"I'm afraid so. We had some excitement in the middle of the night and I left the front door open, and when I got back she was gone."

"Oh, no." He sank to the grooming stool, his eyes filled with dismay. "Oh, I'm so sorry. That's terrible."

"Well, the worst part is she was lost to start with so she has no idea how to find her way back here, and I really don't know where to start looking. But I feel like I should at least try. So if you can manage by yourself here for a few hours, I want to take Cisco out to search the woods, maybe ride up and down the highway to see if I can spot her."

"Maybe she went back home," Corny suggested hopefully.

"I doubt that. Home is Virginia. I think her family was just traveling through."

"Well," he said, trying very hard to be helpful, "if I were a dog and I were lost, the first thing I'd try to do is find my way to the place where I wasn't lost. If only you knew where that was."

"Thanks, Corny, but …" Then I hesitated, looking at him thoughtfully. The Hemlock Ridge Campground was only about five miles from here as the crow flies—or the dog runs. Once my collie Majesty had walked all the way from my house to my Aunt Mart's house in the dark and the rain, and that was practically all the way to town. Golden retrievers are known for their tracking sense; what if Rick had picked her up as she was on her way back to the last place she had seen her folks?

"You know something?" I looked at Corny with a new and cautious appreciation. "You may have a point. It's worth a try, anyway."

I took a business card from the holder on a shelf and scribbled my cell number on the back of it. "I'll bring one of the girls up to answer the phone, but I'll only be gone a couple of hours. Go ahead and start Max's bath, and don't be afraid to call me if you have any questions."

He took the card. "Don't worry, Miss Stockton," he assured me fervently, "I'll take care of everything. I'm just … so *sorry*."

He looked so earnest that I had to smile. "I appreciate that, Corny, but it's not your fault." He really had to learn to stop taking things so seriously. He reminded me a lot of Pepper in that regard. "I'll be back as soon as I can."

I left Katie in charge of the phones, and Marilee, who was, if I had to make a choice, the more responsible one, in charge of the dogs—including Pepper, Mischief, and Magic—in the playroom. I threatened to Tweet pictures of them without makeup across the universe if they were not still here when I got back, and loaded up Cisco into the SUV. I didn't actually have pictures of either one of them, with or without makeup, and I wasn't entirely sure I knew how to Tweet a picture even if I had, but they didn't know that, and the uneasiness on their faces when they heard the threat made me pretty sure they weren't going to try to sneak out early again.

I could hear Cisco's excited panting from the backseat as we made our way up the mountain toward the ranger station. The area I intended to search was actually on the other side of the mountain, but it was protocol to check in. Besides, I owed Rick the courtesy of an explanation about how I'd lost the dog.

But when I reached the ranger station at the top of the mountain, I could tell Rick had bigger problems than a lost dog. The front parking lot was crowded with four sheriff's department cars, including the K-9 unit, and, from the look of the back lot, half the jeeps in the Forest Service had been called in. A half dozen deputies and rangers bent over a topographical map that was spread on a table on the front porch of the rustic log cabin that served as the main office of the ranger station. I could see Jolene, notebook in hand, interviewing a rather harried-looking man in the shade of a picnic shelter a few feet away. The man kept tossing anxious looks at Nike, her gorgeous Belgian Malinois police dog, who sat in perfect attention at Jolene's side, but I could understand his consternation. Most people are a little afraid of police dogs.

I parked on the grass on the opposite side of the road, rolled down all the windows, and told Cisco I'd be back in a minute.

Rick looked up as I crossed the road and waved me onto the porch. "Good," he said, "they called you. I was afraid you wouldn't have time to help."

"Help with what?" I shoved my hands into my jeans pockets as I came up the steps, trying not to look around too anxiously for Buck. It was inevitable we'd run into each other sooner or later, but I really wasn't ready for it yet. "Nobody called me. I'm just here looking for a dog. What happened?"

Rick nodded in the direction of Jolene and the man she was talking to at the picnic shelter. "Fellow says his wife went for a walk last night and hasn't come back. They're in the RV section of the Bottleneck Campground."

I frowned a little. "Kind of hard to get lost over there."

Bottleneck was so named because of the way the nearby creek narrowed and then exploded into a waterfall, but during tourist season its popularity gave the name a double meaning. Throughout July and August the bottleneck of campers sometimes meant a two-hour wait to sign in on the weekends, and the place was wall-to-wall with tents and RVs. The hiking trails were all flat and well marked, and they all led right back to the campground.

Tim White, a deputy I'd known a few years, explained, "We think she might've gotten turned around in the dark, maybe hurt somehow, or met with foul play. Her husband said she didn't have her phone. Did you bring your dog?"

Before I could answer, Jolene said behind me, "That won't be necessary. Nike works best alone."

I lifted my eyebrows and turned to face her. "Two dogs are better than one," I pointed out, as nicely as possible.

"Two dogs only confuse the scent trail," she returned, making no visible effort to be nice.

"Nike is a great dog," I replied, "but Cisco is wilderness certified. And he knows these woods. If you want—"

"Look," Jolene said, sharply enough to make Rick turn and look at her. "I know you're used to being the hot ticket around here, but amateur hour is over. The sheriff's department has its own dog now, and we'll be handling things from now on. Get used to it."

"I'm not an amateur!" I objected, temper flaring. "I'm as qualified as you are, maybe more! Cisco, too!"

Her tone was cool. "Nike is a deputy with the Hanover County Sheriff's Department. We are paid to do this. You are not even qualified to be here."

I drew in an outraged breath, but she cut me off. "This is a police matter, Stockton," she said. "Don't make me cite you for interfering with an investigation. You need to take your dog and get out of our way."

With a flick of her finger she called Nike to heel, and the beautiful dog glided to her side. As much as I wanted to give Jolene a piece of my mind, I certainly could not fault Nike's training. And clearly Jolene considered the discussion to be over. She turned her back on me and bent over the map, addressing the assembled deputies and ranger. "The husband says he thinks she went west. That means she was likely to have taken one of these trails." She pointed on the map. "We'll work in teams of three: two rangers, one deputy. Nike and I will search the deep woods beginning here …"

I met Rick's disbelieving gaze and gave a shrug that I hoped successfully disguised my pique. I was a volunteer, and when a police officer told me to go, I had to go. It was a good thing I wasn't going far, though, because I had a feeling Jolene might be persuaded to reconsider turning down free help before the day got too much older.

"Listen," I told Rick, speaking below Jolene's military-like commands, "I'm going back over to Hemlock Ridge where you found the golden yesterday. I had this crazy idea she might've tried to get back to her family's campsite. I've got my cell phone if you need me."

He muttered, "*When* we need you."

Again I shrugged.

He nodded toward Jolene. "Is her dog any good?"

"The best," I assured him. For sniffing out drugs or armaments or taking down a fleeing suspect on the street. But in these woods ... well, we would soon see.

I turned to go back to my car, and couldn't resist tossing over my shoulder to Jolene, "Call me if you need me. Rick's got the number."

Jolene did not even look up.

By the time I got to the Hemlock Ridge Campground I was feeling irritated, foolish, and more than a little sour. In the first place, Cisco and I had made seven verified wilderness rescues over the past two years, and okay, some of them were so simple they involved little more than pointing a lost hiker back in the direction of the trail, but some of them, like the little girl lost in the woods, were life or death. How many rescues had Nike made? We knew what we were doing. I should have stood my ground with Jolene. I shouldn't have let her just kick us out like that.

On the other hand, who was I going to complain to? Buck?

In the second place, I was clearly grasping at straws to think that Cameo would return to the place she was picked up yesterday morning. Even if she wanted to, what made me think she could find this place again, or that she might have gotten here already? It could take a lost dog days, circling around, trying to pick up her own scent trail. It was far more likely that she would return to my place, which was closer and more recent in her memory, than here.

I almost got back in the car and drove to Bottleneck to join the search for the missing human, but two things stopped me. The first was the fact that, quite simply, I refused to beg Jolene to let me do my job. The second was the eager, hopeful expression in Cisco's eyes as I stood there holding his tracking vest, debating.

I put Cisco's vest and tracking harness on him and let him sniff the baggie of Cameo's hair that I'd taken from the brush I'd used to groom her before bedtime last night. I brushed my hand across the dirt of the road beside which I'd parked and told him, "Track."

He took off enthusiastically but it was clear after a few minutes he had nothing. That might have been because campers kept interrupting us with, "Mommy, look! Can I pet the dog?" and "We have a dog just like that at home!" Some parents were astute enough to point out the vest and tell their children the dog was working, even though Cisco, with his wagging tail and grinning face, looked less like a working dog than any dog I'd ever known. And since he actually *wasn't* working by any normal definition of the word, I told people we were on a training exercise and took advantage of their curiosity to ask everyone we met if they had seen a golden retriever running loose that morning. No one had.

About a mile down the dirt road from the campsite there is an overlook where you can park your car, pose the family in front of the rock safety wall, and take a fantastic photo of a multilayered, blue and lavender, green and yellow, forever mountain view. Curls of fog rising off a distant peak reminded me why it's called a smoky mountain; tracks of old logging roads and animal trails lined with bright red sourwood and sorghum always made me think of the stitching on a crazy quilt. Back when I worked for the forest service and used to patrol these roads in a jeep, this was one of my favorite spots. Sometimes I'd stop for lunch at the picnic shelter to the west of the overlook, and I've taken many a tourist's photo posing with that magnificent vista in the background.

There was a family of tourists posing for a photo now; a blonde-haired mom trying to control two wiggling children on the rock wall while Dad stretched out his arm for the all-inclusive selfie. I was about to volunteer to take the photo for them when suddenly Cisco, who'd been sniffing the gravel walkway for tidbits the kids might've dropped, suddenly stiffened and turned his nose to the air.

It was clear he had scented something, but I couldn't tell from which direction. To the north there was nothing but a tangled gorge so steep you looked down from here onto the tops of trees. To the south was the dirt road down which we'd just come. To the east and west the gorge sloped more gently, but it was still a wilderness. Cisco turned his head, tasting the air with that magnificent nose of his, sorting out the thousands upon thousands of pieces of information he was gathering from it, and then, unexpectedly, he barked.

Cisco is trained to sit and bark to alert me when he has found his target. This is the one thing about which he is very consistent, but unless the innocent-looking tourist family was concealing a big golden retriever somewhere on their persons, he had not found anything. Still, I believed Cisco, and I actually turned to look at their car, wondering if they might have picked up the stray dog, when I heard, from not so far in the distance, an answering bark.

I swiveled my head around just in time to prevent being jerked off my feet as Cisco, following the sound of the bark, raced toward the edge of the overlook and, placing his front paws on the rock wall, peered over. The children, ten or fifteen feet away, laughed and pointed, and Dad no doubt got a great picture. I looked down over the sheer drop in dismay. Cisco barked again, and again an answering bark came from somewhere within that tangled gorge.

It never occurred to me that the bark might have come from any dog other than Cameo. Like I said, I trusted Cisco, and Cisco knew what he was searching for. But even if it wasn't Cameo, any dog who was lost—or perhaps even injured—at the bottom of that drop needed my help. All I had to do was figure out how to get down there.

I needn't have worried. Cisco is a tracking dog, and his nose led me to the western edge of the overlook, where the slope was less intense and, at least at the top, less overgrown. There was a sturdy timber fence which I climbed over and Cisco climbed under; I grabbed his tracking leash on the other side and we began the slipping, stumbling descent into the gorge. I called "Cameo!" and got nothing; Cisco barked, and got a bark in return. I hung onto the branches of saplings and scrub brush to keep from falling as Cisco plowed down the slope, but I knew it was pointless to try to slow him down. It was all I could do to keep the leash from tangling and doing serious harm to us both.

We had gone five or six hundred yards when Cisco suddenly gave such a lunge that he pulled the leash right out of my hands. I didn't even have the breath to call him, so I stumbled after his leaping, scrambling path, keeping up with him mostly by following the shaking of the bushes through which he tunneled. I threw up a hand to protect my eyes from a slapping branch and in the next moment caught a glimpse of two wagging golden tails. I skidded down another ten feet of incline and wrapped my arm around the trunk of a small pine to stop my forward momentum, leaving behind a layer of skin. But I barely felt the burn as I stood there, gasping, holding on to the tree, staring at what was before me.

Cisco had found Cameo and sat proudly beside her, his tail swishing in the dead leaves. He barked, once, to let me know of his success. Beside him, Cameo worriedly nosed at something on the ground. I blinked the sweat from my eyes and refocused, and for another half second I still couldn't believe what I saw. It very much looked like a person, lying tangled amidst the vines and debris on the ground.

I plunged forward, shrugging out of my backpack, and dropped to my knees beside the form. Automatically my hand dug Cisco's toy out of the pack and I tossed it to him, gasping, "Good find, boy, good find!" I had to push Cameo out of the way to see what it was, exactly, he had found.

It was a woman, her pale hair now dark with dried blood, her face a mass of bruises. One leg was twisted at an odd angle, showing breaks in two places, and an arm was pinned beneath her. She was completely still and her skin was cool and dry to the touch. But when I pressed my fingers reluctantly against her carotid artery I felt a pulse, very faint, very irregular, and my own heart leapt. I whipped a space blanket out of my pack and covered her with it, then dialed 911.

"This is Raine Stockton," I told the dispatcher. My voice was a little shaky and I was still breathing hard. "I have an unconscious female on the slope of Hemlock Ridge beneath Scenic Overlook Number 3. She's badly injured and she's lost a lot of blood. I need paramedics and a rescue team, and better have an airlift standing by. And," I added on a last, deep breath, "radio Deputy Smith. I think she can call off her search."

CHAPTER SEVEN

Hanover County may be a small rural community with no real resources to compare to those of big cities, but our Emergency Rescue Response team is second to none. As soon as I heard the sirens approach the overlook, I set off a flare to pinpoint our location, and rangers were clearing a path to us only minutes after that, with EMTs close behind. When the paramedics were on the scene, the best thing I could do was to get out of the way, so I took the dogs back up the newly cleared trail and walked them the mile or so back to my car.

The ambulance was just pulling away when I parked my car at the overlook, rolled down the windows for the dogs, and hurried over to where Rick was helping a couple of deputies string a police tape barrier across the part of the fence they'd had to take down in order to get the stretcher up the slope. I could see Jolene on the radio in her unit, and a gaggle of tourists lined the other side of the road, craning their necks to see whether or not the excitement was over. Rick looked up when he saw me, and I trotted over to him, panting a little as I unscrewed the top of a water bottle. "How is she?"

He gave a small, grim shake of his head. "Alive. I guess that's something. They're going to try to stabilize her at Middle Mercy, and then probably life-flight her to Asheville. Good thing you found her when you did, though. Another few hours of exposure …" Again he shook his head. He added, "You look pretty beat up, yourself. You need some first aid?"

I shook my head and took a long drink from the bottle. "Just part of the job. Anyway, I didn't find her, Cameo did. And Cisco found Cameo." Then, because I could see I was confusing him with irrelevant information, I hurried on, "What do you think happened? I don't see how she could have wandered off the road far enough to fall, even at night. I mean, the fence goes on for almost a quarter of a mile."

"We think she went over the barrier at the overlook," one of the deputies volunteered. "There's a patch of damaged bushes where she might have hit, then continued to fall to where you found her."

Rick and I looked at each other, the unspoken truth clear between us as it must have been to anyone who took even a casual look at the overlook: The rock wall was topped with an iron fence four feet high to prevent precisely that kind of accident. The only way a person could fall from there was if she deliberately climbed over.

Of course, tourists had been known to do stupider things.

I said, "Do we know who she was?"

"Her name is April Madison," Jolene said, coming up behind me with notebook in hand. "I need a statement from you, Stockton, and then we can wind this up."

Rick said, "Thanks for your help, Raine. Give Cisco a biscuit for me." He turned to go back to work but I barely heard him. I was staring at Jolene.

"Madison?" I repeated. "*April* Madison?"

She gave one of her familiar annoyed frowns and glanced at her notebook. "According to her husband. Why? Does that name mean something to you?"

"But—that's Cameo's mom! We were looking for the same person! Well, I mean, you were looking for a person and I was looking for a dog, but ... Oh my God." I pivoted to look back at my SUV where two golden faces, each securely buckled into the backseat, looked out from the open windows. It all made sense now. Cameo had not accidently stumbled upon the injured woman. She had deliberately come back here because she knew where she was. If I were as fanciful as Sonny I might even say she had deliberately tried to lead us—or at least Cisco—here. As a matter of fact ...

Jolene interrupted my flying thoughts with an impatient, "Stop babbling and stick to the facts. Do you know this woman or not?"

My phone rang, and I glanced at it quickly. It was Melanie, but this time I really could not take her call. I pocketed the phone and swung back to Jolene.

"The dog," I returned, equally impatiently. "The stray I took in. I told you about her yesterday, remember? Her microchip has her registered to an

April Madison of Highlands, Virginia. Is that the same woman or not?"

She flipped a page in her notebook, her expression suspicious. "That's right. But the husband didn't say anything about a dog."

"But," I said, frowning as I tried to put together the picture, "I thought you said they were camped at Bottleneck. That's a good five miles away no matter which route you take. How did she get all the way over here?"

"We're still trying to determine that."

I glanced around. "Where is her husband?"

"One of the deputies gave him a ride to the hospital."

I said, "Well, check with Rick, then. Campers have to register their dogs when they check in. But I'm telling you, this is the same dog."

Jolene did not bother to hide her skepticism. "So you're saying the woman went out to walk her dog, walked five miles across a mountain in the dark, and fell over the barrier?"

I had to be careful here, because I wasn't entirely sure what I was saying, and the parts I was sure of, I didn't like. "Well," I ventured, sounding unconvincing even to myself, "it's possible, I guess. Maybe her dog got away. She could have climbed over the barrier if she was trying to get to her dog, and then she slipped and fell. The only thing is," I added thoughtfully, "the dog was picked up early yesterday morning, and she had dried blood all over her coat. Like she had been lying in a puddle of it, maybe all night. Maybe longer."

I tried not to picture that sweet, loyal dog, racing down the gorge after her fallen mistress, desperately trying to wake her, finally lying down beside her and staying there all night, maybe longer, because she didn't know what else to do. Finally hunger, or thirst, or maybe the instinctive need to find people because people, in a dog's world, almost always made things right, had driven her to leave the person she loved. She might even have been trying to find her way back to her own campsite—one RV out of hundreds— when Rick picked her up. I actually had to blink back a sudden sting of tears, but Jolene just stared at me, her face impassive.

"So," I went on, prompting, "is it possible the timeline is wrong? That April Madison actually fell two days ago and that the blood on her dog's coat was hers? And why didn't her husband say anything about their dog being missing as well? And even if you do believe she's only been missing since last night, don't you think it's a little strange that the husband didn't report it until this morning? If someone I loved went walking in the mountains at night and didn't come back, I'd be beating down the ranger station door until I got some help."

She muttered, "Yeah. I did wonder about that." She flipped her notebook closed and started to walk away. Then she glanced back over her shoulder at me. "Why is it," she demanded sourly, "that every time I get around you, things get complicated?"

I lifted my shoulders innocently. She tightened her mouth and shifted her gaze upward in a sharp gesture of dismissal, and continued toward her car.

"Hey," I called after her. "What should I do about the dog?"

Not surprisingly, she did not even turn around.

It was almost two o'clock when I got back to Dog Daze with Cisco and Cameo in tow. Corny was behind the counter, just hanging up the phone, and when he glanced up I actually saw his face lose color. "Is *that* the dog?" he gasped. His eyes looked like round blue globes behind the magnification of the glasses. "The cream golden?"

I unclipped Cisco's leash and he immediately raced over to the counter and placed his paws atop it, gazing hopefully at the treat jar I kept there. I kept the leash on Cameo. "Her name is Cameo," I said. "I'm afraid her owner had a bad fall in the gorge. I'm keeping her until … well, until things are more settled."

I opened the treat jar and tossed Cisco a peanut butter dog cookie, then offered one to Cameo, who took it from my hand more delicately. After all, they had both earned it.

Corny sat down hard on the stool. "But—but I think I know her!" he stammered. "What I mean is," he went on quickly, "I think I saw her with her owner, out walking the other day. Oh, no, that poor lady! She fell?"

I said, "Which day? Where did you see them?"

"Well, I guess it was closer to night. Tuesday, just before dusk. I was riding my bike in the national park, they were going the other way. You don't see many goldens that color outside a dog show, so I noticed." A look of relief crossed his face. "But at least that wasn't when she fell. I mean, her husband stopped and picked them up just as I passed."

"How do you know it was her husband?" I asked. "Had you seen him before?"

He looked confused. "Well, no. But who else would it have been? She seemed to know him, and the dog—Cameo—jumped right in the car."

"Do you remember what kind of car it was?"

"Not really," he apologized. "I'm not very good with cars. It was a regular one. Not big. I wasn't really paying attention."

"What part of the park were you in?" I asked.

Again he looked apologetic. "I wasn't looking at signs. There was a waterfall not far away, though, and a big campground."

"Bottleneck?" I suggested.

"Maybe. That sounds right."

I frowned thoughtfully. If Corny was right, and April Madison had gotten into her husband's car on Tuesday night, it would certainly explain how she got from Bottleneck to Hemlock Ridge. And if, for whatever reason, she had gotten out there and *then* climbed over the barrier—perhaps chasing Cameo— the time line made much more sense. But her husband must have seen what had happened. Why hadn't he reported it?

Perhaps for the same reason he'd lied about how long April had been missing.

I said, "Corny, do me a big favor. I have to go back to town. Could you keep an eye on things for me? And maybe get this girl cleaned up a little? She was a real hero today."

Of course, that left me no choice but to tell Corny the whole story, and I did so as quickly as possible. The fact that it had been his idea to search for Cameo in the place she was originally found seemed to more than make up for the distress he'd felt over learning that the woman he'd last seen healthy and vital was now hanging on to life by a thread. "I can't believe it," he kept exclaiming while I capsulated the morning's adventure for him. "I was right! I can't believe I was right! You found her just where I said! I was actually right! It's like a Lassie story," he went on, rhapsodizing, "only in real life! I mean, Cameo practically led you to her injured owner, and if she hadn't run away last night you never would have found her—the owner, I mean—so it's all pretty amazing, isn't it? I mean, practically a miracle!"

I hated to add fuel to Corny's dramatic fire, but I had to give credit where credit was due. It had been his idea to search Hemlock Ridge, and if I hadn't done so, April Madison might not have been found until it was far, far too late. As for Lassie … well, I'm not exactly a fan, since I believe that particular collie set an impossibly high standard for every dog who came after her and made my job—as well as that of other dog trainers around the world—more difficult, but I have to admit, in this case the comparison was justified. Cameo's devotion, not to mention her uncanny intelligence, had saved her mom's life. I've been in this business for a long time and it's nice to know I can still be surprised.

I left Corny brushing the burrs out of Cameo's coat while I ran to the house to shower off the blood and smudges and change into clean clothes. Cisco, who was having one of the best days of his life— having not only made a successful find but been reunited with his best friend—stayed in the grooming room to admire Corny's work.

There were two messages blinking on my machine as I raced through the kitchen on the way to the shower. Impatiently, I pushed the "play" button. The first one was from Aunt Mart.

"Raine, honey, I know you're busy, but I wonder if you'd have time to stop by here today or tomorrow before you go down to the fair. I don't know how, but I got put in charge of the church raffle and I have the quilt we're raffling off as a prize here. It sure would help me out if you could run it by the booth for me, since you're going to be there anyway. And don't forget I've got that piece of pie for you. Bye-bye now." She added, "Oh, and the tomatoes. Don't forget those! Love you, sweetheart. Bye."

Family. You've got to love them.

The next message was more surprising.

"Miss Stockton, this is Marshall Becker. We met yesterday at the diner. I have some information you might be interested in, if you'd give me a call."

He left his number, but I didn't write it down. Seriously, some people. I hurried upstairs to shower and change.

I consider myself a responsible person, I really do. But sometimes it just seems as though I have too much to be responsible for. I still had to set up for tomorrow's agility class, and I had four pickups this afternoon, not to mention the grooming clients and the day care dogs. But I really needed to talk to April Madison's husband about Cameo, at the very least to let him know I would be happy to keep his dog as long as he needed me to. Besides, I was curious about what had really happened to April, and I could be sure Jolene wouldn't bother to keep me informed.

So I was definitely in a quandary about leaving my business—not to mention my own dogs—in the care of two teenage girls and a first-day employee whose references I hadn't even checked. But this was an emergency, and if I hurried I might still be back in time to check out the final boarders and close out the books for the day. I changed into a skirt and blouse that I thought would be suitable for a visit to the hospital, grabbed a pair of sandals, and ran down the stairs, pausing at the coat rack in the kitchen to snag my purse. At the back door I paused to put on my shoes, hopping a little for balance, and my bare foot came down on something piercingly sharp. I gave a yelp and grabbed the doorknob to keep from falling as I bent to see what I'd stepped on. It was a small gold pin in the shape of what looked to be a schnauzer, and the post of the pin had left a small drop of blood on the ball of my foot. The dog pin looked like something Melanie would collect; she must have dropped it the last time she was here.

Then I remembered the call from Melanie that I'd let go to voice mail. I had forgotten to call her back. Not to mention her father. I winced with regret and vowed to call them both the minute I got back. I dropped the pin into the zippered pocket of my bag for safekeeping, wiped the blood off my foot, and put on my sandals. Then I hurried across the drive to ask one more favor of Corny.

"You're going to leave Cisco with *me*?" Corny pressed a hand to his chest as his eyes once again went big behind the white glasses. "Oh, Miss

Stockton, I'm honored! I promise I won't let him out of my sight! I'll treat him like my own! I'll—"

"Actually," I interrupted, "if you'll just put them all in the playroom like you did yesterday they'll be fine. I'll try to be back before five and ..." I looked at him apologetically. "I know you came in early and now you're staying late, and of course you'll be paid for the extra hours but if you want time off tomorrow ..."

He waved it away. "Don't be sil! There's no place I'd rather be. Anything I can do, anything at all, to make your job easier ... Well, I mean, you saved a woman's life today, you and Cisco!"

"And Cameo," I added modestly, although it was nice to be appreciated.

We were in my office, with both Cameo and Cisco, now freshly brushed and sprayed with coat-shine, milling about my legs, no doubt looking for the treats I perpetually kept in my pockets. The skirt did not have pockets, and I had stopped keeping treats in my purse after the dogs had chewed holes in two of my favorite ones. I took a couple of dog biscuits from the bin on a high shelf, asked for a sit, and gave each golden retriever a well-earned biscuit. I spotted Cameo's collar where I'd left it on my desk and put it on her, then dropped the little tracking button into my purse. Those things were not cheap, and I wanted to return it to her owner before I lost it.

I arrived at Middle Mercy hospital a little after three o'clock. I am not wild about hospitals, having been through too many crises there with too many people I loved, some of whom never left. I intended to make this visit as quick as possible, and when I caught a glimpse of a sheriff's department uniform through the glass window of the ER waiting room, I didn't bother to stop at the information desk, but went straight through the swinging door to where Jolene was talking to a haggard-looking man I vaguely recognized from the campground earlier. He looked to be in his fifties, though dark-circled eyes and sagging cheeks made him look older. He had a bald spot on his head and a scruff of grayish beard on his cheeks. He kept pulling at the whiskers as he talked, as though the beard bothered him.

There were only a couple of other people in the waiting room, and they cast furtive, curious glances at the man and the police officer, trying to overhear their conversation. But neither Jolene nor April's husband noticed me as I approach. I heard him say, "I told you, I don't know anything about that." And I slowed my steps so as not to interrupt.

Jolene said, "Mr. Madison, it might have helped our search if we'd known your wife had gone out looking for her dog. Why didn't you mention that?"

"What difference does it make?" He looked agitated, pulling again at his face. "If it hadn't been for that stupid dog none of this would have happened."

I definitely slowed my step then.

Jolene glanced at her notebook. "So you say the dog disappeared two days ago, right after you checked in. Did you report it to the park ranger?"

He looked annoyed and impatient. "What is all this about the dog? It's my wife I'm worried about!"

"We're just trying to determine what happened, Mr. Madison."

He replied shortly, "No, I didn't report it."

"But you kept looking for the dog every day."

"April did. She made us stay an extra day because of that mutt. We're supposed to be in California by the twentieth. I told her we didn't have time to waste. We have a schedule to keep." His voice caught on a little break, and he rubbed his whiskers vigorously. "Had," he corrected tightly. "Had a schedule to keep."

Jolene paused respectfully for just a moment, then said, "Would you describe your wife as an athletic type? Someone who might go under a guardrail and try to climb down into a gorge?"

"For God's sake, the woman is fifty-two years old and twenty pounds overweight." His voice had an edge to it. "No, I would not describe her as athletic."

I know it's not smart to judge people by their most stressful moments, but I was starting not to like Mr. Madison. By this time I was standing behind Jolene, and I thought it might be a good time to speak up. "Not even if she saw her dog down in the gorge and thought she could reach her?" I said.

Jolene turned to scowl at me, and I moved around her, extending my hand to the man. "I'm Raine Stockton," I said. "I'm the one who found your wife."

"Tony Madison." He shook my hand with a brief, dry grip. "Thank you," he added, and shifted his gaze away.

I could see Jolene was about to say something to me, so I went on quickly, "Actually, it was your dog, Cameo, who found her. I just found Cameo. In fact, I found Cameo twice. The first time was yesterday morning, and then she got away from me. I think she knew your wife was hurt and she was trying to get back to her." Tony Madison was staring at me as though I might well be a lunatic, and Jolene's impatience was growing. I hurried on, "She has a microchip. Cameo, that is. We've been trying to reach the telephone numbers that are listed but of course no one answers at your home phone. Do you have a cell phone?"

He said, still staring at me, "What?"

And Jolene said, sounding annoyed, "Stockton, you're interrupting."

I ignored her. "Because I'm happy to keep Cameo until things are, you know, more stable for you, but I need your contact information. We tried calling the alternate contact number …" I searched my memory for the name. "A Mr. Sellers? But it's been disconnected."

Now I had his attention, and he did not look pleased. "Greg Sellers? That's who she put down?"

I nodded. "Who is he?"

"April's ex-husband." He frowned uneasily. "She got the dog in the divorce."

I nodded again. It's not unusual for a new spouse to resent a pet from a former marriage, but I still didn't think it was any excuse for calling Cameo a "stupid dog," particularly when she was anything but. "I guess she didn't get around to changing the contact number," I suggested. But she had managed to change her last name on the contact information when she remarried. Interesting.

He said, "Look, Miss …"

"Stockton," I supplied.

"Right." He looked around distractedly. "Miss Stockton, I appreciate what you did, but this is not a good time."

"I understand," I assured him, and dug into my purse for my cell phone. "If you could just …"

Behind us a voice said, "Mr. Madison?" and he jumped to his feet. Jolene stood as well as the doctor approached.

The doctor said, "Mr. Madison, we've done all we can for your wife here, and we're getting ready to air-lift her to Asheville. There's a neurosurgeon standing by. His name is Dr. Richfield, one of the finest available. It's possible they'll take her into surgery tonight, or first thing tomorrow morning."

"Can I see her?" Madison demanded.

"She's unconscious," the doctor replied, "but if you want to step in for a moment before they take her out, the nurse will show you the way."

Tony Madison hurried toward the waiting nurse, and the doctor started to turn away. Jolene stopped him. "What's the condition of the victim?" she said.

He shook his head grimly. "Not good. Frankly, I'm surprised she made it this far. There was considerable blood loss from the head injury, leg and arm fractures, broken ribs, severe dehydration and exposure. She must've been lying there two or three days …"

Both Jolene and I seized on that, but Jolene said it first. "Are you sure? The report we have says she went missing last night."

He gave a dismissing shake of his head. "Then the report is wrong. The color of the contusions alone tell us they're at least forty-eight hours old, and the muscles had already begun to contract around the broken tibia. She's been in that gorge a lot more than twelve hours, Deputy. A lot more."

When the doctor was gone I turned to Jolene in grim triumph. "Told you."

"Go home, Stockton," she said, pulling out her phone.

"There's something else you should know," I said, ignoring her. "My new employee was near the campground Tuesday night and he thinks he saw April and Cameo get into the car with Tony Madison."

"He's her husband. There's no reason she shouldn't."

"Except that her husband said the dog had been missing since they checked in. And he only thought of that after you asked him about the dog, right? And if she did get into his car, it would explain how she got all the way over on the other side of the mountain."

Jolene scowled at me. "What makes you think the person your so-called witness saw was April Madison?"

"The dog is pretty distinctive," I told her. "White."

"All right, I'll talk to him. Now will you get out here?" She pushed a button on her phone.

"I didn't get Mr. Madison's phone number," I objected, pivoting around to look for Tony Madison.

Jolene propped the phone between her shoulder and chin while she scribbled in her notepad. I heard her say, "Sheriff, I need permission to take a couple of men and do a more thorough search of the accident site at Hemlock Ridge."

I could almost hear Buck say, "What're you looking for?" And even imagining the sound of his voice made my shoulders tense.

"Signs of possible foul play," was Jolene's response, and I looked at her more intently. After another moment she said, "Yes sir, I do." And "Thank you."

She disconnected and tore a sheet of paper out of her notebook, thrusting it at me. "Madison's cell number," she said. "Now, go."

She strode past me toward the exit, and I lost no time making my way to my own car.

CHAPTER EIGHT

My aunt's house was on my way home, so it would have been foolish not to stop. If I didn't linger, I could still make it back in time to check out the boarders at five. Before I left the hospital parking lot, though, I called Dog Daze, mostly just to make sure someone was actually answering the phone. Katie did.

She assured me everything was fine and then added, somewhat sotto voce, "The new guy is organizing all the cream rinses by coat color and making bows out of that paw print ribbon you keep in your office. I didn't know if that was okay or not. He's kind of funny, isn't he?" she added in an even lower, somewhat uneasy tone.

I said, "It's fine, Katie. And Corny is just eccentric, that's all." I tried to sound more confident about that than I felt. "He's been a big help and I'm lucky to have him."

"Well, in that case," she said in her normal voice, which was perky with just a hint of wheedling, "it's my grandma's birthday tonight and the family is having a big get-together, so I was wondering if I could go ahead and leave? I have to, um, help with the cake."

Translation: she had a big date and she needed to do her nails. I scowled at my watch as I turned the key in the ignition and rolled down the windows to let some of the heat escape while the air-conditioning kicked in. "It's only three thirty."

"Please? I promise I'll make it up next week."

I sighed. "Get Marilee to answer the phone and you can go."

"Oh, she left at two, remember? You said she could last week. But the new guy said he didn't mind taking care of the phone."

I did not remember telling Marilee she could leave early, but the longer I argued about it the longer it would take me to finish my errands and get back to work. "All right," I told her impatiently. "Tell Corny I'll be back in forty-five minutes."

"Yes, ma'am. Thank you!"

I disconnected the phone, looking forward to the time my part-time summer help returned to school.

I was surprised to see an unfamiliar bright red pickup truck in my aunt's driveway, the extended cab kind that men around here drive when a car would have been more practical, just because real men drive pickups. I parked beside it and got out curiously. I had to blink when I saw Marshall Becker sitting with my Uncle Ro on the front porch, both of them drinking lemonade.

"Hi there, Rainbow." Uncle Ro got up to give me a one-armed hug as I came up the steps. "Your Aunt Mart said you might be coming by. Do you know Marshall Becker?"

Becker, who had gotten to his feet when I approached, extended his hand. "We met yesterday. Good to see you again, Miss Stockton."

I shook his hand and said suspiciously, "What are you doing here?"

"Marshall's been helping me out from time to time with a case," Uncle Ro explained. He had recently formed a cold case squad for the three adjoining mountain counties. "He's still a consultant with the state police, you know. It's good to have him back in town." He looked at me more closely. "What'd you do to yourself, sweetheart? Been tangling with a bobcat?"

"Pine tree," I explained. "Cisco and I were on the search for that missing woman this morning." I didn't have to explain much more than that; my uncle kept his police scanner going day and night, and there was very little that went on in this county he didn't know about.

He nodded. "Should've figured. How's she doing?"

"Not good. They're life-flighting her to Asheville. I have her dog. Oh, no," I muttered as I suddenly remembered. "I forgot to give this back to the husband."

I unzipped the pocket of my purse and took out the little electronic button, showing it to my uncle. "It's a GPS for dogs," I explained. "Pretty fancy, huh? They had tried to sew it into her collar but the stitching came loose. Those things cost a couple of hundred dollars."

My uncle examined the button with an appreciative grunt, and then passed it to Marshall. "Looks like the same kind of transmitter people use to bug offices."

Marshall turned it over between his fingers, frowning as he held it up to look at the underside. "It is," he said. "It's exactly the kind of bug people use to listen in on conversations, only better. Look at that."

He tried to show my uncle something on the underside of the button, but Uncle Ro shook his head. "My glasses are in the house. What does it say?"

"It's a KD-620. We just got word on these things at the department last year. It not only tracks movement and transmits sound, it also records conversations in case you lose the transmission. The FBI used one of these to catch a kidnapper a couple of months back."

I said skeptically, "Why would anybody want to put a listening device on a dog? It's not as though she'd have a lot to say."

Marshall Becker gave me an amused look, and my uncle supplied, "I imagine they were more interested in what the people around the dog had to say. Pretty clever, come to think of it," he added with a thoughtful nod. "Nobody would ever suspect the dog. What do you suppose it was doing there?"

"I don't guess it's illegal for a private citizen to have one," Marshall admitted. "A man suspects his wife of having an affair, a businessman suspects his partner of double-dealing ... lots of reasons. And like you said, no one would look twice at the dog hanging around."

"Wow," I said, staring at him. "Cameo was a spy."

Becker smiled. "Or it could be they were just using it as a GPS, like you said. You have to program it to activate the voice transmission and record feature. I have a friend at the department who's an expert in this kind of high-tech stuff. Do you want me to ask him to take a look at it?"

"No," I said, scowling as I held out my hand. "No, I don't. It's not mine. And unless it's illegal, I have to give it back."

He gave a small shrug and returned the button to me. "Suit yourself. But if I were you I'd go in the kitchen right now and get a piece of aluminum foil to wrap it in. You do realize somebody could be recording every word you say."

I looked at him suspiciously, and sure enough, his eyes were twinkling. "I've got nothing to hide," I replied, and dropped the thing back into my purse. "Aunt Mart's waiting for me."

I went immediately to the big country kitchen, which was redolent with the aroma of peanut butter cookies. Aunt Mart was just taking a tray out of the oven, and she smiled over her shoulder to me, her cheeks flushed with the heat. "I thought that was you I heard pull up, honey. Pour yourself a glass of lemonade while these cool."

Majesty the collie, who watched regally from her plush bed in the corner, deigned to rise and come over to greet me. I dropped to my knees and gave her a hug, burying my face in her sweet smelling fur. Majesty had been my collie from the time I'd rescued her from poverty and neglect as an adolescent pup until I came to realize last year that my Aunt Mart needed her more than I did. I still thought of her as my dog, but, although Aunt Mart and I pretended to share custody, I think we both knew where Majesty's heart was.

"Thanks, Aunt Mart," I said, giving Majesty a final long stroke with my fingers as I stood. "But I can't stay. I've got half a dozen dogs waiting to go home this afternoon so I have to hustle." I opened a drawer and pulled out the aluminum foil.

"Well, it won't hurt you to sit down for a minute. Gracious, what happened to your arm?"

So I explained the story of the rescue all over again while I wrapped the transmitter in foil. Better safe than sorry, I suppose.

Aunt Mart clicked her tongue and gave a small shake of her head as she lifted the cookies on to a cooling rack. "The work you do, child," she said.

I wondered what kind of work Tony Madison did, to have access to a device like this—or to know someone who did. It was definitely worth looking into.

I went to the sink to wash my hands, knowing full well I wouldn't be leaving this kitchen without eating something. "So when did Uncle Ro become such goods friends with the opposition?" I inquired, trying to sound casual. "I thought he was a Lawson man all the way."

"Ro is a politician all the way," she corrected. "He has friends in every camp."

She offered me a warm, melty peanut butter cookie on a paper napkin, and I took it. Sheer heaven.

I poured a glass of milk from the carton in the refrigerator and helped myself to another cookie from the cooling rack. "Are you entering anything in the county fair?"

"Oh, gracious no. Who has the time?"

We chatted a few minutes about the fair while I ate more cookies and Aunt Mart packed up a package for me that included leftover grilled chicken, key lime pie, a dozen cookies, and a basket of tomatoes. I love that woman.

"You chop up that chicken with some tomatoes and lettuce and make yourself a nice salad for supper," she told me. "Do you have lettuce?"

I assured her that I did, though I wasn't entirely sure, as I gathered up the goodies. "I hate to eat cookies and run, Aunt Mart, but I just hired a new guy to help run the kennel and I've already left him alone all day. I need to get back and see how he's doing."

"You did?" She beamed at me. "Well, good for you! Now maybe you can have weekends off every once in a while like a normal person. Anyone we know?"

"No, he's from out of town. He seems great, though." I hesitated. "Maybe a little too great," I admitted. "As in, too good to be true."

"Oh, honey," she said, sighing. "I wish you could learn to trust people more. Sometimes the good Lord knows what he's doing, don't you know?"

Easy for her to say. She didn't know anything about listening devices in dog's collars and men who lied about their wife's disappearance and ... well, men who lied. And I couldn't tell her that the last man I'd trusted had been a crazed bomber who'd almost killed us all.

I hugged her and kissed her on the cheek. "Thanks for all the food, Aunt Mart. I'll make sure the quilt is in the booth before lunch tomorrow."

She carried the quilt in its plastic dry-cleaning bag while I carried all the food she'd packed, and Marshall Becker immediately got to his feet as we came out onto the porch. "I'll take that for you, Miss Mart," he said, reaching for the quilt. "I was just about to leave."

Aunt Mart pressed a container of cookies on Marshall Becker, who certainly didn't try very hard to object, and we spent a few more minutes saying good-bye. Marshall walked me to my car, carrying the quilt. When we were out of earshot of the two on the porch he said, "I left a message for you."

"I got it."

"I wasn't sure you'd want me to say anything in front of your uncle," he went on, "but I kept an eye on that guy that was hanging around your car yesterday ..."

I shot a surprised look at him.

"And when he got into his own car—which was two blocks away and didn't look anything like yours, by the way—I ran his tag number, just out of curiosity."

Now I stopped and stared at him. "Terrific," I said. "As if this country didn't have enough troubles, now we have to worry about bored ex-cops running our tags just for fun."

He gave a small lift of his eyebrow. "I thought you might be interested in what I found out, particularly in light of ..." He inclined his head back toward the house, referencing our last conversation. "Recent events. But if it offends your sensibilities ..."

"Oh for Pete's sake." I opened the back of the SUV, put the groceries inside, and turned to take the quilt. "What?"

"The guy was not a reporter," Marshall responded, "or a tourist. He was a private detective."

I stopped stone still, staring at him. "A what?"

"I just thought you'd want to know, since even I have to admit his behavior was a little suspicious. Do you know anyone who might be investigating you?"

I felt my cheeks go cold, and then hot. There was only one person I knew who had the money and the means to do something like that. But I happened to know that Miles had run a pretty thorough background check on me months ago, before he ever introduced me to his daughter, and he'd been completely upfront about admitting it. I'd been furious at first, mostly because around here if we want to know everything there is to know about someone we ask a neighbor, not a PI, but after a while I'd realized he was only trying to be a good dad. So if it wasn't Miles ...

I hated myself for thinking it, tried to talk myself out of it, but ... could it possibly be his ex-wife? And if so, was she, too, just trying to protect her daughter? Or was she sizing up the competition?

I could feel my teeth clenching with anger, and I made a conscious effort to loosen them. "Does he have a name?" I demanded. "A phone number?"

"I have that information at home," he said. "I'll call you."

I took the quilt from him and laid it in the back of the SUV, pushing aside a dog-hair covered blanket and readjusting a crate to make room for it. I took my time, willing my cheeks—and my temper—to cool. Then something occurred to me and I straightened up, turning back to Marshall.

"This guy," I said, "this PI. What kind of car was he driving?"

"A Honda Accord," he replied without hesitation. "Dark blue." He must have seen the change on my face because he added, "Why?"

"I thought someone was following me yesterday," I said, frowning a little, "in a dark blue sedan. And last night I had a prowler. I'm pretty sure the car I saw was a dark blue sedan."

His attention quickened. "Did you call the police?"

I shook my head. "The dogs scared him off before he could do anything. There was nothing to report."

He looked disturbed. "If it was the same guy, he could lose his license for that kind of thing." And then he tilted his head slightly, looking at me with new interest. "You do lead an interesting life."

"Yeah, well." I slammed the door on the SUV and walked around to the driver's side.

He walked with me. "You're going to be at the fair tomorrow?"

"I'm manning a booth."

"Maybe I'll see you there. I'm judging jams in the morning and giving a speech in the afternoon."

"Of course you are." I opened the door and got inside.

He placed his hand on the door before I could close it. "By the way," he said, bending down to look at me, "that thing about the aluminum foil is a myth. I'd get rid of that bug as soon as possible if I were you."

I rolled my eyes a little and put the car in gear. But as soon as I reached the end of the driveway I ripped the foil off the little device, tossed it in the glove compartment, and locked the door. Maybe I didn't have anything to hide, but that didn't mean I wanted some stranger listening to everything I said, either.

Of course, the first thing I wanted to do when I got home was call Miles and demand an explanation for the private investigator who was following me— or at least to find out what he or his ex knew about it. But there were already two cars in the Dog Daze parking lot, and for the next hour Corny and I ran an assembly line of check-outs: I greeted the owners and passed Corny the leash with the checklist of toys and personal items the pup had brought in; I took the payment and told the owners how perfect their dog was; Corny brought the dog and all its luggage to the front and told the owners how perfect their dog was; humans, dogs, and personal belongings went happily on their way, I posted the check and we started all over again. It felt a little like a fast-food restaurant, but we got the job done with an absolute minimum of chaos, and in record time.

When the last day care, grooming, and boarding client who was due to be picked up that day had, in fact, been picked up, I gave Corny a weary high five and told him he could go home.

"I don't mind staying for the evening feeding," he insisted. "It would take half the time if both of us did it."

I was mightily tempted, but I had to draw the line somewhere. "Thanks, Corny," I said firmly, "but you've been here all day. Go home and get some supper. I'll see you in the morning. Ten o'clock," I added as I turned to go back to my office.

I thought he hid a flicker of disappointment behind a quick smile. "Yes, ma'am," he said, "I'll be here. Do you want me to bring your dogs up from the playroom before I go? They were all absolute angels while you were gone."

I doubted that very much, but it was nice of him to say so. "That'd be great, Corny, thanks."

I turned on my computer and brought up the course map I intended to use for tomorrow's agility lesson in sequencing. While I waited for it to print I glanced through the messages Katie had left rather untidily on my desk. There were two cancellations for class, which suited me just fine since they'd paid in advance and this meant I would be finished sooner; a couple of call-back requests for information on private lessons, and a message from a Professor John Rudolph with nothing but a telephone number.

At first I didn't recognize the name, then I remembered. Corny's reference. I called him back on my cell so that he would have that number, and I got voice mail again. I left another message, this time with all my telephone numbers, and hung up just as the click of claws and the panting of happy dog breath

arrived outside my door. Corny had all five of my
dogs on leashes walking in a perfect trot at his side
and looking more pleased with themselves than I had
ever seen them. I laughed out loud in delight and
amazement and of course that broke the spell. Corny
released the leashes and the herd thundered toward
me, butts wriggling and tongues lolling. Even Cameo,
who was new enough to the pack to still be shy,
joined the fray. I got down on my hands and knees,
opened my arms, and let them bowl me over.

All right, all right, I know. But I'd had a hard day.

Corny looked on with a benevolent smile while I
ruffled fur and dodged wet doggie kisses and
struggled to keep my balance while twenty paws tried
to climb all over me. "Well then," he said, "if you're
sure you don't need me ..."

I scrunched up my face as Pepper's tongue got
me across the eye. "Thanks, Corny. I appreciate all
your help today, really. See you tomorrow."

I gave each of the dogs a last big hug and got to
my feet. That was when I noticed the employment
papers I'd left for Corny to fill out that morning were
still on my desk, untouched. I snatched them up and
hurried after him, calling, "Hey, Corny!"

I reached the front reception area just in time to
see him pedaling down the drive. He had left his
windbreaker hanging on the coat rack beside the
door—an easy mistake to make since it was close to
ninety outside this time of day—and I went to tuck
the papers into a pocket so he wouldn't forget them
tomorrow. Something was already in the first pocket I
tried, and it pricked my finger when I reached in. It
was a baseball cap, neatly folded and tucked inside the

pocket, and I pulled it out a few inches, smiling a little, just to see what it was bedazzled with.

It was not, however, covered with rhinestones or sequins as I'd expected, but with dozens of tiny gold pins. Dog pins, just like the one I'd found on my kitchen floor that morning.

I went over to my purse, found the little gold schnauzer I had stored there for safekeeping, and compared it to the ones on the cap, frowning. Sure enough, it was just like the others. I could even see the little hole in the fabric where it had fallen off. So how had it gotten in my kitchen? Or perhaps more accurately, when had Corny been in my house? And why?

It was starting to look as though I was the one who needed to hire a private detective.

CHAPTER NINE

I felt bad about leaving the dogs alone most of the day—especially Pepper, who was a guest, after all. Cameo was still exhausted from her adventure and seemed content to snooze in her crate, and Cisco was content to be stretched out on the floor of the playroom beside her, chewing on a bone, so I took Mischief, Magic, and Pepper to the agility yard and let them run the five-obstacle sequence I had set up for tomorrow's eight-o'clock class.

For Mischief and Magic it was child's play, of course; they were both seasoned competitors, and Magic had come very close to winning high in trial earlier in the season. But watching Pepper scramble over the A-frame and take the low jumps with her big, flat-footed puppy leaps, ears flying and face grinning, made me laugh out loud with pure pleasure and momentarily drove all those buzzing, annoying, and unrelated questions out of my head. Like who would hide a transmitter in a dog's collar, and why?

And when had Corny been in my house and why hadn't he mentioned it to me? Who was he, anyway? And, easily the most disturbing question of all: Why had April Madison's husband lied about how long she'd been missing? Unless, of course, he had a reason for not wanting her found.

And of course there was the whole question of who had hired a private detective to follow me.

I fed the dogs, made myself a tomato sandwich and a glass of iced tea, and took my cell phone out onto the front porch, where the shadow of the mountain and the whirling ceiling fan reduced the temperature by five or six degrees. While I ate, I could at least start to track down the answers to some of those questions.

I put up a gate to block off the steps to the front yard, and all five dogs came outside with me. Mischief and Magic immediately chose the coolest corner of the porch and flopped down to snooze. Cameo stretched out at the other end of the porch, panting mildly as she gazed over the dusty fading day. She had done her job, and she seemed satisfied with it. Pepper nosed in the wicker basket of dog toys—one of several such baskets I kept strategically located around the house—and came up with a fleece tug toy, which she immediately took to Cisco, inviting him to play. Cisco grabbed the other end of the toy, played tug with her for about ten seconds, and had no trouble winning. I tried hard not to laugh when he took his prize over to Cameo and laid it at her feet. She ignored him. Pepper went back to the basket for another toy.

My phone had been off since before lunch, and I saw that, in addition to the call from Melanie, there were three missed calls from Miles, but no messages. Most intriguing, though, was a missed call from Jolene—again no message. She had never called me before, for any reason. I didn't even know she had my number. I called her back first, and got voice mail.

I gave my name and said, "Did you mean to call me? Because your number was on my phone. Anyway, if you did, call me back. I'm here."

Next I took from my pocket the crumpled piece of paper on which Jolene had scrawled Tony Madison's cell phone number, and I dialed it. I got voice mail. I said, "This is Raine Stockton. We met earlier at the hospital. I'm the one who, uh ..." This was where it got awkward. "Found your wife in the gorge. I hope everything is going well. I have your dog, remember? I know you have a lot to deal with right now so I just wanted to let you know not to worry about Cameo. I have a boarding kennel and I'll keep her as long as you need me to. I just wanted to leave my number for you. Just be in touch when you can." I left my telephone numbers and disconnected.

I took a bite of my sandwich and dialed my own voice mail next, calling up Melanie's message.

The minute I heard her voice I knew something was wrong. I swallowed quickly, my throat tightening even as I did so. "Raine," she said. Her voice sounded breathless and shaky, as though she was upset or scared and trying not to be overheard. "Don't call me back. I'll get in trouble. My dad says ..." Now her voice went high and tight and wet with tears. "My dad says I can't talk to you anymore! I'm not supposed to

… supposed to call you, but I had to tell you …
Please tell Pepper I love her! I don't know if I'll ever
see her again! I have to go." Her voice caught once
more on a sob. "Bye." Then, tearfully, "Don't call me.
Bye."

My hands were shaking so badly that if I had had
to push more than two buttons I probably wouldn't
have been able to do it. Miles answered on the first
ring. "Raine," he said, but I barely let him get the
syllable out.

"Oh!" I exclaimed, my voice sharp with sarcasm
and feigned surprise. "So you're allowed to talk to me,
but Melanie can't? Good to know!" He tried to say
something but I sucked in a breath and barreled on,
"How *dare* you? How dare you tell Melanie she can't
talk to me! I don't care what's going on with you
down there, but I'm her friend—maybe her only
friend! She was crying, Miles, she thinks she's never
going to see Pepper again. How could you do that to
her? How *could* you?"

"Raine," he said, "it's not what you think."

"And that's another thing." I couldn't stop myself
now. My emotions were like an avalanche, catapulting
downhill and carrying me helplessly along with them.
"If you want to get back with your ex that's fine. Do
what you want, I can't stop you. But the least you
could do is be man enough to tell me! You don't have
to be such a damn …" My voice was suddenly thick
with tears and I swiped angrily at my eyes. "Sneaky,
coward about it!"

Miles said lowly, "What in the *hell* are you talking
about?"

I drew in a single steadying breath, willing my tone to sound even and reasonable. I was unsuccessful. "I mean, I understand. She's Melanie's mother. It's probably the best thing for her. Maybe for everybody. We never made any promises to each other. That's not what this is about."

His voice sounded cool. "Is that what we've been doing this past year? Not making promises to each other?"

I cried, "It's just ... how could you tell Melanie not to call me? How could you take Pepper away from her? How could you?"

I stopped talking, mostly because I was afraid that anything else I said would be completely unintelligible. Miles let the silence go on for a beat, and then another. Maybe he was counting to ten. Maybe he was waiting for me to.

He said, "Are you finished talking like an idiot?"

I said nothing, shifting my gaze to the sweet goldens across the porch from me. Cisco nudged the tug toy closer to Cameo. She ignored him. Pepper nipped playfully at Cisco's tail. He ignored her. I didn't even smile.

"I know Melanie was upset," Miles said. "I've already talked to her. She knew something was going on between her mother and me and she misunderstood, but I've explained things to her now. She knows she's not going to lose Pepper. I didn't tell her she couldn't be your friend. I just asked her not to call you for a while. I wanted to talk to you first."

I felt that cold, sinking feeling in my stomach again, that hollowed-out, sucker-punched feeling. "So it's true," I said dully. "You're going back to your ex-wife."

He made a rough sound of stifled exasperation. "What in God's name put that in your head, I'd like to know! In the first place, that would be the worst possible thing I could do for Melanie. She'd be an orphan inside a year because her mother and I would kill each other long before that. In the second place, I can't think of anything in this world I want to do less. I don't even like the woman."

"Then why—"

"Oh, for the love of ..." He blew out an exasperated breath. "I'm not breaking up with you, Raine. I'm trying to keep you out of a lawsuit!"

The breath went out of my lungs and I sat back hard in the chair. "*What?*"

Across two continents, I could almost see him thrusting his fingers through his short, spiky hair, tightening his lips, choosing his words. The only thing I'd ever known that could upset Miles's equilibrium was Melanie, so I think I knew what he was going to say before he said it.

"Melanie's mother has been in touch with her lawyers in the States," he said finally. "She's suing for full custody of Melanie by trying to have me declared an unfit parent."

I gasped. "But—she can't do that! That's absurd, Miles, how can she say that? You're the most devoted father I've ever known. No court is ever going to believe her. It's ridiculous!"

"Thanks, sweetheart." His voice sounded tired, almost grim. "But I'm afraid the court might not see it that way. The fact is that ..." He seemed reluctant to go on, but he must have known there was no point in delaying the inevitable. He finished, "Since she's been with me, Melanie has been interviewed by the police at a drug bust, she's been kidnapped, and she's been held hostage at gunpoint. I don't know. Maybe her mother is right. Maybe Melanie is better off with her."

I felt my fingertips start to tingle, and my cheeks grew cold. It was a moment before I could even speak. "But ..." The word came out as barely a croak and I tried again. "But none of that is your fault! Those things ... those things all happened because of me. Oh Miles," I whispered as the full weight of the truth sank in. "You're going to lose your daughter because of me."

"Raine, that's not ..."

"Oh my God." I caught my breath. "*That's* what the private detective is about. That's why she's having me investigated!"

"What are you talking about?" he demanded sharply. "What private detective?"

"Miles," I said quickly. "Miles, listen to me." My breath was coming fast and light, and so were my words because I knew if I didn't get them out quickly they would lodge in my throat and choke me. "You can't see me anymore. I can't be in Melanie's life. I'm the one who's a danger to her, not you. You can't lose Mel. You have to break up with me. There are lots of other women out there. You'll find somebody better. But you have to ..."

"Oh, for God's sake," he muttered.

I hurried on, "You know it's true. It was never going to work out between us anyway, we're just too different, and it's not worth it. Nothing is worth losing Melanie …"

"Raine, stop talking," he said harshly, and I did. "We're not having this conversation now. I'm not losing my daughter. I'm going to deal with this, but first I have to get her out of this damn country. I'll talk to you when I get back. In the meantime, could you not do anything rash? Could you do me that one favor and for once in your life not do anything rash?"

"Miles …"

"When I get back," he repeated firmly, and he disconnected the phone.

I sat there, staring at the phone in my hand, not entirely sure what had just happened. I started to call him back, but what I would say? I had just broken up with him.

Hadn't I?

The phone rang in my hand and I jumped, instinctively pressing the "accept call" button and answering a little breathlessly. I was so sure it was Miles that I didn't even understand the meaning of the first few words that were spoken.

"Stockton," the woman's voice said brusquely. "Jolene Smith from the sheriff's department. The sheriff said I should call as a matter of professional courtesy to inform you of the status of this morning's victim, Mrs. April Madison. I'm sorry to say she succumbed to her injuries at 14:35 this afternoon."

I blinked, trying to focus. My voice was hoarse. "What?"

Jolene replied, "She didn't make it."

I said weakly, "Oh." Unbidden, my gaze moved to Cameo. She was sleeping now, her head resting on the floor boards next to Cisco's, untroubled. She had done her best.

Jolene seemed to hesitate and then said, "We found blood on one of the posts at the overlook. We're waiting for forensics, but if it turns out to be Madison's we'll be opening a homicide investigation. I'll be out to interview your employee in the next day or two about what he saw at the campground. Meantime, you'll let me know if you remember anything that could pertain to this case."

I pulled my gaze away from Cameo, trying to concentrate on what Jolene had said. "Um, wait a minute," I said. "There might be something."

"What?" she demanded, rather impatiently.

I rubbed the bridge of my nose, trying to massage away the headache that was forming there. "Do you remember I told you about the dog? April Madison's dog?"

"Stockton, I don't have time …"

"She had a tracking device in her collar," I went on, speaking over her. "At least, I thought it was a tracking device. Turns out it was a transmitter. You know, like a bug."

She was silent for a moment. When she spoke her tone was skeptical. "In the dog's collar."

"That's right."

"How do you know what it was?"

"I showed it to my uncle. You know, the former sheriff?" I couldn't resist that one. "He was with Marshall Becker. He's the one—"

"I know who he is," Jolene broke in, annoyed.

"Anyway, he said it's the kind that not only tracks and transmits, but also records. I was thinking that if

Tony Madison suspected his wife of having an affair, he might have planted the bug to prove it. And if he got the proof ..."

"That might also be motive for murder," Jolene murmured. Then, briskly, "I'll need to take the device into evidence. Where is it?"

"I still have it." I glanced at my watch. "I can bring it by the office in about half an hour. I have to run an errand for my aunt first." I hadn't really planned to go back out today, but if I dropped the quilt off at the fairgrounds on my way into town it would save me a trip in the morning. Besides ... I looked unhappily at the remainder of my sandwich, my appetite now completely gone. I had nothing better to do.

She seemed to debate for a moment whether the best use of her time was to follow protocol and drive all the way out in the country to collect the evidence from me, or to bend the rules a little and allow me to bring it in to her. Then she said, "Half an hour." She disconnected.

I don't usually take the dogs with me on rides this time of year, but after losing Cameo once I was not at all comfortable leaving her at home alone. It went without saying that I couldn't take Cameo anywhere without also taking Cisco, so I crated Pepper, Mischief, and Magic, loaded up Cisco and Cameo in the backseat of the SUV, and started for town.

To me, there is nothing prettier than a lighted Ferris wheel at dusk, and the sight of it turning so gracefully against the blue-gray sky as we approached the fairgrounds was enough to soothe my jangled nerves. Tonight was opening night of the county fair, and even though the contest judging and entertainment events wouldn't officially begin until tomorrow, the parking lot was almost full when I pulled in. I showed my pass and drove around the dirt path to the lot that was reserved for staff and volunteers. It was located behind the carnival attractions, on the edge of a wide weedy field that was surrounded by woods.. There were a some equipment trailers and supply trucks parked at the far end of the field, where they would remain until the fair closed down next weekend. I parked in the shade behind the carousel, rolling down all the windows halfway before I got out. The sound of calliope music and the smell of popcorn floated in through the open windows and suddenly I was hungry again. Suddenly I missed Miles, and Melanie, so intensely that it hurt.

I had no time to feel sorry for myself, however. The temperature had dropped to the seventies, which felt cool after the scorching day, but I knew the dogs would not be comfortable in the car for very long, and Jolene was waiting for me. I shook off the emptiness with a single deep breath and got out.

"Five minutes, guys," I promised, and I hurried around the car to get the quilt out of the back.

As I closed the door and punched "lock" on my key fob—which was a little silly, since anyone could just reach inside and unlock the doors—I remembered the evidence in my glove box. It was locked, of course, but with the windows open it didn't feel secure to me. So I went back, removed the little button from the car, and tucked it securely into the zippered pocket inside my purse. "Five minutes," I repeated to the dogs, relocked the car, and left at a trot.

It could not have taken me more than five minutes to find the church booth, admire the display of crafts the Women's Auxiliary was selling, and help Mrs. Whitaker hang the quilt with clothespins from the rope that had been strung across the back of the booth. She thanked me all the while and assured me I didn't have to make a special trip, that tomorrow would have been soon enough, and I assured her it was no trouble at all and I was happy to help. I made my escape with a wave and a promise to stop back by tomorrow to buy something.

I paused to wave at Sonny, who was working the Humane Society booth with Hero, and called, "Can't stop! Dogs in the car!" She waved back, sending me on my way, and I walked quickly back toward the car.

There was a crowd at the carousel and I edged my way through, holding on to the strap of my shoulder bag. Shrill-voiced children bounced up and down, pointing toward the horse they wanted to ride while moms and dads jostled for their places and tried to keep their cool. There was a guy in a red-striped hat hawking bags of peanuts, and one of the Rotary Club men, dressed in a tuxedo, moved through the crowd doing magic tricks with coins and cards. I saw the clown, but I paid him very little notice. I saw a lot of things.

I had mostly made my way through the press and was headed toward the dirt path that led toward the back gate when someone bumped me hard. I started to turn and then someone grabbed my purse. I yelled, "Hey!" and grabbed back, whirling. I had a brief, startled glimpse of fuzzy red hair, a polka-dot bow-tie, a clown mask, and then my legs were kicked out from under me and I went down hard in the gravel.

When I looked up the clown, and my purse, were gone.

CHAPTER TEN

"I already told you," I said to Mike, the deputy who was interviewing me. I winced as the paramedic dabbed at my bloody knee with an alcohol-soaked pad. "He was wearing jeans and a tee shirt of some kind. A polka-dot bow tie that looked like it was part of the clown face. And it wasn't a regular painted-on clown face. It was a mask, like …"

"Like this one?" Deke, one of Buck's top deputies, pushed into the small first-aid tent with a latex mask in his hand, complete with attached fuzzy red wig and a sewn-on yellow polka-dot tie.

"That's it!" I brushed away the ministrations of the paramedic and got to my feet excitedly, barely restraining myself from reaching for the evidence. "Where'd you find it?"

"They sell them at a booth right near the entrance." Deke ignored me and spoke to Mike. "We found this one in the trash can next to the corn-dog stand."

"See if anybody saw the man who threw it away," Mike said.

"Maybe the owner of the booth remembers who bought it," I suggested, and Mike gave me a barely tolerant look. Most of the guys at the department liked me okay, but none of them appreciated it when I tried to help them do their jobs. Besides, this was a purse snatching, not a homicide, and I guessed they wouldn't spend a whole lot of time trying to solve it. There would probably be a half dozen more before the fair was over.

The paramedic who was in charge of the first-aid tent said, "Do you want me to wrap that for you?"

I could only guess it had been a slow night for him. "I'm not six," I replied impatiently. "It's fine." And then I added, because I knew I sounded rude, "Thanks." The truth was, I had had ACL surgery on that knee last year and it really hurt. I limped a little as I moved toward the front of the tent. I saw someone approaching who made me very unhappy, and I looked at Mike.

"You radioed this in?" I said accusingly. "You couldn't wait until your shift ended and write a report like a normal person?"

Now he was starting to look annoyed. "It's procedure."

The paramedic said, "You should get a tetanus shot."

I waved him off distractedly. "I'm up to date." In my line of work I got a tetanus shot every year whether I needed it or not.

Jolene drew up before me, hands on her utility belt, glowering. "I might've known." She looked me up and down, then turned to Mike. "What happened?"

Mike looked uneasy, as he often did in the presence of Jolene. "Looks like a simple purse snatching to me. Deke's out talking to witnesses, but we don't have much. I didn't know they were going to call in the K-9."

But even as he spoke Jolene swiveled her head back to me, her nostrils flaring, her gaze boring a hole through me. She said lowly, "Don't tell me."

"Well, what I was supposed to do?" I shot back. "I was on my way to bring it to you! How did I know someone was going to steal my purse?"

She turned sharply back to Mike. "This is a priority. I want that thief. More importantly, I want the purse."

Mike hesitated. He and Deke were assigned to the fair and had caught the case; she wasn't his boss. He made the mistake of sounding a little too condescending as he said, "We're doing what we can, Deputy, but you know as well as I do the chances are pretty slim. Most of the time it's just a random thing, some kid …"

She muttered, "Oh, for God's sake."

Jolene swung away to say something into her radio, and Mike gave me a small shrug. He was getting no sympathy from me, though. This might be a routine matter to him, but it was *my* purse that had been stolen.

My spirits rose considerably when I stepped out of the tent and saw Sonny approaching on her motorized scooter. She was dressed in an ankle-length, flowered gauze skirt and wore her silvery hair in a long braid over one shoulder, with amethyst chandelier earrings that brushed her shoulders. She looked as regal as a gypsy queen, riding sidesaddle on the scooter, and people moved aside when she passed. Hero, in his red service dog vest, trotted along beside her, and on the other side were two gorgeous golden retrievers. There weren't many dogs who would have walked so calmly through the crowd beside a motorized vehicle, and I was proud of the goldens for showing such good manners.

Still, I didn't want to take a chance of causing an accident, so I waited until she brought the scooter to a stop before I hurried forward to take their leashes. "What good dogs!" I exclaimed. I bent to hug them, because kneeling was impossible. "Great dogs!"

"They were fine," Sonny said. "I gave them some water, but they were in the shade and didn't seem the least overheated."

Sonny had been one of the first to arrive after bystanders pulled me to my feet and called 911. It was she who had insisted I go to the first-aid tent, instead of trying to chase down the thief as I had originally intended. I'd agreed only on the condition that she check on my dogs. Besides, even I knew that by then the thief was long gone, along with all my credit cards and cash.

"Thanks, Sonny." I smiled at her gratefully as I straightened up, mostly because she understood that, after what had just happened, I wasn't so much worried about the dogs' comfort as I was just worried about them.

She said, concerned, "Are you okay, Raine? You look like you were mauled by a bear."

I shrugged. "I'll live." And then my expression sobered as I glanced down at Cameo. "Her owner, the woman I found this morning in the gorge, didn't make it."

"Oh, how awful." Her voice, and her expression, were filled with sympathy. Her gaze traveled to Cameo as well. "What's going to happen to that beautiful dog?"

"I'll try to call her dad again when I get home," I said, "although I hate to bother him at a time like this. I guess she'll go home with him ... if Jolene doesn't arrest him first."

She shot me a surprised look. "Really? Do the police think he was involved?"

I was about to answer when Cisco, who had been happily sniffing the ground with Cameo for dropped popcorn and other goodies, suddenly looked up, ears arcing and eyes alighting with excitement. I gave him a quick correction with the leash in anticipation of what I knew was about to happen, because as I always tell my students, the time to intervene is before your dog makes a mistake, not after. He all but ignored me, and, even more remarkable, ignored Cameo, who looked up from her sniffing to regard him curiously. There was only one person who could make Cisco act that way; only one person he loved as much as, if not more than, me. Sheriff Buck Lawson.

I wound an extra loop of leash around my hand and Cisco whimpered with joy, panting and grinning, as Buck approached. I heard Buck say to Jolene, "That won't be necessary, Deputy." He held up something to her, and I saw he had my purse in his hand.

Buck glanced at me, and I could see the blue mark that my hand had left across the top of his cheek bone. Cisco rose up on his back legs, pawing at the air, and Buck, noticing him, almost smiled. I stiffened my shoulders and set my jaw as he started toward me. Jolene followed a few steps behind.

Buck nodded at Sonny, "How're you doing, Sonny?"

She replied pleasantly, "I'm fine, Buck. Surprised to see so many men working on a purse-snatching, though."

"We don't like to see this kind of thing get a handhold, first night of the fair and all."

That was what he said. I think he came because he'd heard my name on the radio. He always came when he heard my name—not because of any particular tenderness, but because of some stupid machismo sense of responsibility that, over the years, had become a habit. Once Mike had told me that they had standing orders to notify the sheriff whenever a call came in from me, because I was family. That might've been true when my uncle was in charge, but it was clear Buck needed to make some changes. Especially now that he was married.

Buck handed my purse to me. "We found it in the Dumpster behind the ticket stand. Everything looks like it's there—phone, driver's license, credit cards, forty-two dollars in cash?"

I passed the dogs' leashes to Sonny and grabbed my purse. Buck bent to rub Cisco's ears, and I thrust my fingers into the zippered pocket inside. It was empty.

I looked at Jolene and she read my face. "Great," she muttered.

Buck straightened up and looked at her. "What?"

Jolene said, "Sir, Stockton found what she thought might be a micro-transmitter in the collar of the dog belonging to the Madison woman. I asked her to bring it in for examination, and apparently it was stolen."

Buck scowled. "A micro-transmitter? In a dog's collar?" He looked at me. "What made you think that's what it was?"

"I didn't," I replied coolly. "Uncle Ro and his friend Marshall Becker did. Marshall said he'd seen something like it used by the FBI."

I have to say, it gave me a certain amount of pleasure to toss Becker's name around so casually. And I enjoyed the way Buck's eyes darkened with questions he was not permitted to ask when I did.

Buck turned on Jolene. "Let me get this straight. You discovered a piece of sophisticated surveillance equipment on a dog belonging to a dead woman and you didn't think that might be pertinent to our investigation?"

Jolene said stiffly, "Yes sir, I did think it was pertinent. That's why I wanted to take it into evidence."

"But you can't, can you?" His tone was sharp. "Because now it's been stolen. Why didn't you go and collect the evidence yourself, Deputy?"

She tightened her lips and raised her chin in the instinctive manner of a soldier accepting discipline, and I knew she wouldn't defend herself. I said, "Because I volunteered to bring it in. If you ask me . . ."

Buck shot me a glance. "I'm not asking you." He demanded curtly, "Check your purse again. Is anything else missing besides the transmitter?"

I checked again. I'm not one to carry around a lot of stuff—my wallet, cell phone, some dog pickup bags, an extra clicker. It was all there. "No. Nothing but the transmitter."

His frown deepened. "The guy knew what he was looking for then."

"Sir," Jolene volunteered, "there's no reason to think the device wasn't still active. If it was, the thief may have tracked her here."

"Good heavens," said Sonny uneasily.

I had to agree. Creepy.

Buck turned back to Jolene. "Finding this thief is your top priority. I want all the witness reports on my desk by end of shift." He cast a last, scowling glance at me and added, "Get someone to escort Miss Stockton back to her car."

"Yes, sir."

But he was already striding away.

I took the dogs' leashes from Sonny. "I don't know about you," I said, "but I think I've had enough fun for one day."

She nodded agreement and looped Hero's leash around the handlebar of the scooter. "I'm parked next to you," she said. "I'll go with you. You need to go home and take care of that knee."

We started toward the midway and Jolene fell into step beside us. I said, "I don't need a police escort."

"I have my orders," she replied, and I tried not to roll my eyes.

"Anyway," I said, trying to be gracious, "I'm sorry you got in trouble. He only yelled at you because he couldn't yell at me."

I sensed her sharp intake of breath and thought she was going to make a typical retort. But the words that came out were a rather grudging, "I'm always in trouble with him."

I murmured, "I know the feeling."

We moved onto the midway, where the crowd had grown even more now that the sun had fully set. The air was filled with the ping of carnival games and the squeal of children as they sailed by on the tilt-a-whirl; the call of barkers hawking hot dogs, peanuts, and cotton candy; the pervasive, nostalgic sound of calliope music. People smiled and pointed when they saw the parade of dogs, and a little girl almost lost her cotton candy when she lingered too close to Cisco. She was close to Melanie's age, and I smiled at her even as I spoke sharply to Cisco and pulled him close.

Then, unexpectedly I got a lump in my throat. I missed Melanie. I missed Miles. I missed them so much I couldn't even think about them, so I blinked away the hot blur in my eyes and started to say something meaningless to Sonny. That was when one of the goldens at my side leapt to the end of the leash with an outburst of excited barking that was interspersed with hopeful, high-pitched whines. It sounded just like Cisco when he anticipates a really tasty treat and loses control ... or when he sees Buck. In fact, I was so sure that the culprit was Cisco that I automatically scolded, "Cisco, quiet!" while I reeled in the leash. Cisco, who was already at my side, gave me a puzzled look. The barking and whining was coming from Cameo, and she was as animated as I had ever seen her.

I pulled her back to my side and she swiveled her head around, still barking, although it was beginning to sound a little forlorn now. I turned to follow her gaze, searching the crowd for whatever it was that had set her off. Another dog? A stray cat? I couldn't think of anything else that would get her so excited and, as hard as I tried, I couldn't see anything, either.

Cisco gave a couple of supportive barks, but it was clear he didn't know what he was barking at, and when I told him to sit, he did. So did Cameo, who had apparently lost track of whatever had set her off. She was still panting with excitement though, and her eyes were bright, as though for the first time she was expecting good things in her future.

"I wonder what that was about," I said, bending down to stroke her ears. "She's usually such a quiet dog."

Sonny regarded Cameo with a puzzled expression, and then she looked at me. "She says," she replied, "it was her dad."

I lifted an eyebrow, and Jolene said, staring suspiciously at Sonny, "What?"

But there was no way I was explaining that to Jolene. I gave a dismissing wave of my hand and said, "Nothing."

Sonny looked amused as I slapped my thigh to get the two goldens by my side and started walking again. But now she'd planted an idea in my head that I couldn't stop thinking about. I hadn't gotten that much of a look at Tony Madison, but the man who'd attacked me had been roughly the same size. And if he'd been the one who had stolen my purse, what better way to evade detection than to simply dispose of the mask and the purse and blend into the crowd again, acting like an ordinary fairgoer until the police moved on?

I said to Jolene, "So did Tony Madison go back to Virginia, or is he at the campground tonight? Because he didn't answer when I called his cell phone earlier."

Jolene said, "His wife just died. Are you really surprised he didn't answer a phone call from a stranger?" She stepped in front of the dogs and me when we came to a corner and I saw her look right and left; it wasn't showy, just instinct. She added, resuming her stride, "Last I heard he was staying overnight in Asheville to make arrangements for his wife's body to be returned home."

I said, "Do you know what he does for a living?"

She replied impatiently, "It's not my job to give you information about our investigation, Stockton. Where are you parked?"

"In the back. Employee parking." She made the turn at the carousel and I added, "I was just wondering if he was in the tech field."

"He's a CPA." And then she paused and gave me an intense look over her shoulder. "Why? Do you have some reason to think he was the one who stole that transmitter?"

"No," I said carefully. Except that Cameo had never barked like that before, and I would stake everything I knew about dogs on the fact that she had just seen someone she knew, and loved. "It's just that he did lie about how long his wife had been missing. And whoever planted the device had to have easy access to Cameo's collar, like someone who lived with her would. And the only person who could track the device would be the one who planted it, right? I mean, if he was following me."

She did not reply, and I prompted, "You're going to see if he has an alibi for tonight, right?"

We had reached my car and I beeped the remote control to unlock the doors. "Because if he *did* plant the transmitter to spy on his wife, that could be the whole foundation of your case," I went on. "It makes sense he'd want to get it back before it went into police custody."

Jolene turned to me. "Let me ask you something, Stockton," she said, looking thoughtful. "Just how stupid are these folks at the Hanover County Sheriff's Department, anyway?"

I was confused. "What? What makes you think …"

"Because to hear you talk," she went on, "you'd think not a one of them ever went to police academy or took the certification exam or even watched an episode of CSI. Well, the good news is, I've done all those things, and I know how to work a case. If I need help from you, I'll be sure to let you know."

She turned to Sonny, whose lips were tight with repressed amusement, and said politely, "Do you need any assistance, ma'am?"

Sonny replied, equally as politely, "No thank you, Officer. I can manage."

Jolene walked away, and I muttered, "I was just trying to be helpful."

I put the dogs in my SUV and helped Sonny with the scooter. Hero jumped into the front seat and Sonny got behind the wheel of her car. "Are you sure you don't want someone to take your shift at the booth tomorrow?" she said. "You've had a rough couple of days."

I said, "Thanks, but I'm good. I'm kind of looking forward to doing something normal for a change."

She said, "Well, you need to take care of yourself. Go home, draw a cool bath, have a glass of wine, and call Miles. He always makes you feel better."

She was right; he did. I felt my stomach clench as I said, "I broke up with Miles."

The dismay on her face seemed to reflect my own. "Oh, Raine," she said. "I'm so sorry." She added, "It's none of my business, of course, but the two of you seemed so good together. And Miles ..." She hesitated, and then said, "I've known him off and on through the years, and I've never known him to be so devoted to anyone. I thought ... well, it doesn't matter." She smiled, though her eyes seemed to search mine as she looked at me. "It's just that ... I know you've got to be a little gun shy after Buck, and ... are you sure this is what you want?"

I heard myself saying, with a shake of my head, "No. It's not what I want at all. It's just ... complicated."

She looked at me with genuine sympathy. "Raine Stockton," she said. "You work harder at getting what you don't want than anyone I know. If you put even a fraction of that energy into getting what you *do* want, you'd be unstoppable."

I prickled at that and wanted to object, but Sonny started her engine. "Let me know if you change your mind about tomorrow," she said. "I'm home all day."

She waved as she drove off, and I lifted my hand in a feeble reply, still frowning over what she had said.

CHAPTER ELEVEN

I slept restlessly and awoke once again the middle of the night, sweating and gasping from the nightmare in which everything I loved in the world was about to be blown out of existence. Instinctively I grabbed my phone and checked for a message from Miles, but there wasn't one, of course. The hollow emptiness in my stomach settled in again as I realized that this time the nightmare had come true.

Almost. Cisco, sensing my wakefulness, rested his sweet golden head on the side of my bed and I dropped my hand atop it, stroking his ears. I lay there staring at the darkness, feeling the steady reassurance of my dog beside me, until the sound of blood roaring in my ears was silent. Night shadows swirled and lightened, and eventually I fell again into an uneasy sleep. But I was glad when daylight came.

I checked my phone again, I don't know why. Nothing. That was fine. That was okay. It only meant that he had thought over what I'd said and come to realize I was right. It was better this way, for everyone. No long discussions, no regrets, no drawn-out good-byes. Much better.

My knee was stiff and swollen, and it took me twice as long as it usually did to get dressed and feed the dogs. I couldn't have been more annoyed with myself. I should have let the paramedic wrap it last night; now I was going to miss most of the fun of teaching a class—showing off how well my own dog and I could do the exercises—and so was Cisco.

I wrapped the knee myself in an elastic bandage and limped around the house for another half hour or so, working out the stiffness. In the summer months, agility class starts at eight a.m. to avoid the heat of the day, which can be dangerous for both dogs and humans when they're running and jumping full speed. I have an air-conditioned indoor training room which I sometimes use for beginning students, but it's too small to set up a sequence class. Besides, running outdoors is a lot more fun, for both dogs and the people. It was clear, however, that I would not be running very far today.

By the time I got to the kennel at seven a.m., Corny was already there, scooping out kibble into stainless steel bowls in the kitchen. The kennels had of course been cleaned and most of the dogs were enjoying the morning air in their outdoor runs. I stopped at the door to the kitchen, staring at him, and he turned quickly, bubbling over with apology and enthusiasm. "Oh, Miss Stockton, I know I'm not supposed to start until ten, but I noticed on the schedule that you're teaching a class this morning, and

I thought if I got here early and took care of the
kennel I might be able to watch? Only if it's okay with
you, of course. I mean, I'm not trying to run up my
hours, this is completely on me, it would just mean so
much to be able to see in person how you work."

I didn't answer. I couldn't answer, because I was
frantically trying to remember whether, when I had
searched my purse for the second time last night, the
little gold miniature Schnauzer pin had been there. I
had put it in my purse before I left for the hospital.
But I hadn't seen it after Buck returned my purse to
me. What kind of thief would ignore credit cards and
cash in favor of a little gold dog pin?

Obviously, the same kind of thief who would put
a transmitter in a dog's collar and then steal my purse
to get it back.

At my continued silence, Corny added anxiously,
"Unless I'd be in the way." Then, "Of course I'd be in
the way, I shouldn't have asked. I'll just get these dogs
fed …"

"No," I said, "no, it's okay. You're welcome to
watch a class any time. Not a problem." Then I
added, forcing a quick smile, "Nice hat."

He stood there beaming, a stainless steel bowl of
kibble in each hand, his fuzzy orange hair poking out
on either side from beneath the baseball cap that was
covered with gold dog pins. He said, "My grandfather
collected the pins, one for each breed he put a
championship on."

"Wow," I said. "Impressive. Looks like there's
one for just about every breed there."

"Just about," he agreed cheerfully.

Except the one for the miniature schnauzer, I thought, because try as I would, I did not see the little schnauzer pin on his hat. I added casually, "Did you find the employment papers I left for you last night? I put them in your coat pocket so you wouldn't forget."

Something flickered across his eyes, but it was too quick, and too subtle, for me to define. "Thanks," he said, and gestured toward the door with one of the dog bowls. "I guess I'd better start serving breakfast."

I moved out of his way and the alarm in his face was genuine as he noticed my stiff movements and bandaged knee. "Oh no! Are you hurt?"

I shrugged it off. "A hazard of the profession. I'll tell you what, though. I'm all for saving steps today, so why don't I fill the bowls and you can distribute them?"

"Absolutely," he assured me. "Whatever you need. You can count on me."

I smiled. "I know I can, Corny." I made my way over to the counter and picked up the list of boarders with special meal requirements while Corny hurried toward the door. "Oh, by the way," I added over my shoulder, as though it were of no importance whatsoever. "Did you happen to go up to the house yesterday while I was gone?"

He turned and looked at me, wide-eyed. "What, your house? No, of course not. Why would I do that?"

I shrugged, pretending to study the list. "It must've been one of the girls, then. I just wanted to mention that if you ever need anything from the house the back door is almost always unlocked during the day. I don't mind if you go in. Just let me know."

"Oh," he seemed puzzled. "Okay."

"Oh," I added, still very casually, "I keep forgetting to mention that the police will probably want to talk to you about what you saw at the campground the other night."

I was certain I did not imagine the flicker of alarm in his eyes. "Police? Me?"

"You know, about seeing Cameo and her owner get into the car."

"Oh." He still looked worried, but then the prospect of being interviewed by the police didn't usually fill anyone's heart with joy. "Well, yes, of course. Whatever I can do to help."

He walked on down the corridor with the two bowls in hand, and I thought his step was a little less carefree than before.

Clearly, I needed to work on my interrogation technique. My father used to say that the only way to get the right answers is to ask the right questions. The problem with that, however, is that there is a very real danger of finding out something you don't want to know. Corny was not only the best employee I'd ever had, he was very likely the best employee *anyone* had ever had. The man had come in four hours early, off the clock, and was doing extra work just so that he could watch me teach an agility class, for heaven's sake. I'd be crazy to look that particular gift horse in the mouth.

Wouldn't I?

Nothing starts the day off right like watching a class filled with really talented dogs doing their very best for their handlers, and I have to admit the agility students that Saturday morning outdid themselves. Corny stood on the sidelines, as delighted as a kid at the circus, occasionally bursting into spontaneous applause when a dog completed a particularly tricky sequence. I knew how he felt. I myself have been moved to cheers and applause when Cisco finished a difficult serpentine jump pattern or followed a blind cross into the tunnel. It's an exciting game.

Every time a dog knocked over a bar Corny would dart forward to replace it, saving me the effort of doing so, and then race quickly back out of the way; the perfect assistant. Afterwards he pelted me with questions about training techniques and the rules of the game which I was more than happy to answer. I love teaching, and who doesn't have a soft spot for someone who is fascinated by what she does best?

Moreover, by the end of the second class my knee had limbered up and I was moving almost normally, so it was turning out to be a good morning. I even brought Pepper down from the house and let her demonstrate how to cross the puppy A-frame, which seemed to cheer her up considerably. Like her young handler, Pepper liked to be the center of attention, and Cisco had not exactly been making her feel special lately.

Happy dogs and tired handlers were making for their cars by 10:00 a.m. when I dashed back to the house to check on the other dogs. I had left Pepper in the day care room with a Boston terrier and two longhaired dachshunds—and Marilee, of course, who'd shown up only five minutes late. The rest of the pack greeted me with their usual outrageous enthusiasm, claws scrambling, butts wiggling, happy breaths panting, and even Cameo pushed her way forward for a greeting. But they all knew Pepper was having fun and they weren't, and they made it pretty clear that there would be a mutiny if I left them alone in the house again.

"All right, all right, guys." I couldn't help laughing as I bent to scratch ears and chins and kiss wet noses. "We're going to play, I promise."

But before we did, I had to check on one thing. I got my purse from its hook by the door and sat down at the kitchen table. I turned the bag upside down and let the contents spill out onto the checked placemat before me: wallet, keys, pickup bags, clicker. My phone was in my pocket. I unzipped all the pockets and shook the bag. A tube of lipstick and a roll of breath mints hit the table, but nothing else. I went through my wallet, just in case I'd misremembered where I put the little dog pin. There were two quarters and eight pennies in the change pocket, forty-two dollars in bills, and that was all.

"Damn," I whispered out loud, and Cisco, who had been trying to tempt Cameo with a stuffed squirrel, looked over at me curiously.

I sat back heavily, puzzled and defeated. Of course I didn't want to believe that Corny had stolen my purse, even though he'd obviously lied about being in my house. I could have sworn the man who attacked me was bigger than Corny, but I knew victims' memories in cases like this were often inaccurate. More importantly, it just didn't make sense. Whoever took my purse was after both the transmitter and the schnauzer dog pin. But the transmitter I'd taken from Cameo's collar had been lying around unsupervised on my desk all day yesterday; Corny could have easily taken it at any time if he'd wanted it. And if he had gone to all the trouble to steal the pin back, why hadn't he put it on his hat? For that matter, why would he even wear the hat around me, knowing that I'd immediately recognize where the pin had come from? The whole thing was just crazy. But I couldn't forget the alarm on his face when I'd mentioned the police, and what had he been doing in the park Tuesday night anyway? Was it possible Corny had been the last person to see April Madison alive?

He still hadn't filled out the employment papers, and Buck had once told me that a surefire method for spotting a kid with a record was when they hesitated about filling out a job application. They didn't want to answer the question, "Have you ever been arrested?".

I was still sitting there, scowling at the contents of my purse, when the ringing of the phone made me jump. At first I instinctively reached for the cell phone in my pocket, and just as instinctively felt my heart skip a beat because it might have been Miles, or Melanie. I realized that the ringing phone was mounted on my kitchen wall at the same time I remembered how unlikely it was that Miles, or Melanie, would ever dial my number again.

"Raine," said the male voice when I answered, "this is Marshall Becker, getting back to you with the information you wanted on that PI. I hope I'm not calling too early on a Saturday morning."

It took me a moment to remember what information he was talking about, and when I did remember I almost told him I wasn't interested. After all, what difference could it make now? I already knew who was behind the investigation, and chances were that, now that I was no longer in Miles and Melanie's life, she would call it off. But curiosity got the better of me, as it almost always did, and I said, "Oh, right. Thanks. What did you find out?"

"The fellow operates out of Virginia," said Marshall, and my attention quickened. "His name is Greg Sellers."

I gasped out loud. "Greg Sellers?" April Madison's ex-husband. The contact person on Cameo's microchip registration. "Are you sure?"

"That's what it says. Why? Do you know him?"

"Um ..." My thoughts were spinning. "No. Not really. It's just that his name came up in connection with a lost dog I'm fostering."

"Well," said Marshall, "that's good news, isn't it? The guy probably wasn't interested in you at all, just looking for his dog."

"Yeah," I said slowly. "Yeah, maybe. Is there a telephone number? The one I had was disconnected."

"It may be the same one." He read off the numbers and I copied them down quickly on the back of a grocery receipt I pulled from the trash.

"Thanks, Marshall," I said. "I appreciate you going to all this trouble."

"Nice to know a lady with flexible opinions. Yesterday you said it was an invasion of privacy."

"Oh." I could barely remember what he was talking about. "Right. Well, it was for a good cause, I guess."

He chuckled. "See you at the fair later?"

"Probably."

"Maybe I'll buy you a corn dog."

"Okay, "I agreed absently, "maybe."

He chuckled again and said good-bye. I cradled the receiver and stood for a moment staring at the telephone number on the back of the receipt. Then I picked up the phone again and dialed. I was surprised when it actually rang through, and surmised—or more accurately, hoped—it was his cell phone.

I have to admit I wasn't entirely sure what I was going to say, and I only had the length of the automated voice-mail message to compose my thoughts. I said, "This is Raine Stockton. I think you know who I am and why I'm calling. I'd like to talk to you about your ex-wife, and about her dog Cameo. I'm working a booth at the county fair today so I might be hard to catch at home, but you can call me on my cell phone."

I left my number and wondered what the odds were that someone who had been covertly following me and who had actually tried to break into my kennel in the middle of the night would bother to return my phone call.

But at least it was starting to make sense now. A private eye would be far more likely to have access to sophisticated surveillance equipment than an ordinary citizen. He had not been trying to break into my car—at least not necessarily—he'd just followed the GPS on Cameo's collar. The same was true of the kennel. The collar, and the transmitter, had been in my office. He'd probably thought Cameo was in the kennel with the other dogs, and maybe he had intended to liberate her, retrieving the transmitter in the process. The question, of course, was why he had planted the device in the first place. I couldn't think of a single good answer for that one.

I did, however, have an idea about who might.

Once again I dialed Tony Madison's number. To my surprise, he answered. "Miss Stockton," he said, apparently reading my name on the caller ID, "I was going to call you about the dog." He sounded exhausted and distracted. "I'm good for the bill. I just have a lot to deal with right now. I appreciate everything you've done, but you don't have to keep calling."

"I'm not calling about Cameo," I said quickly, before he could hang up. "I'm sorry to bother you, I really am, but you mentioned your wife's ex-husband the other day. Greg Sellers?"

There was a surprised silence. Then, "What?"

"Did you know he was here? In Hansonville, I mean."

This time the silence was longer. It was so long, in fact, that I thought he might have hung up. I prompted, "Mr. Madison?"

He said in a quiet, constrained voice, "What are you talking about?"

"The thing is," I said, "I found a listening device in Cameo's collar and—"

"A *what*?"

"It's like an electronic bug. I was going to return it to you, but I think Greg Sellers may have stolen it." He was silent, so I prompted, "I was wondering if you might know anything about it, or ..."

He interrupted harshly, "I don't know what you're talking about, and I don't want to know. My wife just died. All I want is to go home."

"I know, and I'm sorry. I shouldn't have bothered you. If there's anything I can do …"

"I'll tell you what you can do," he said shortly, "you can give me back the damn dog and stop bothering me. I'm at the campground."

I said, "I can be there within the hour."

He replied, "Good." And he hung up.

I replaced the receiver and looked over at Cameo, who was stretched out on the kitchen floor with a pile of Cisco's toys in front of her. Cisco sat beside her, watching her adoringly. Cameo was not only an angel, she was a hero. How dare he call her a damn dog?

But she was his dog, now that April was dead, and I had to return her to him.

Of course, that left me with another problem. If I left now to take Cameo to the campground, it would be a tight squeeze to get back here in time to pick up Cisco and make it to the fairgrounds in time for the dog show and, immediately following, my volunteer time at the Humane Society booth. I didn't need Cisco to help with the dog show, of course, but all of the booth volunteers had agreed to bring their own well-behaved pets because people were much more likely to come over to pet your dog and subsequently leave a donation in the jar than they were to simply wander by and pick up a brochure if you were sitting there by yourself. Besides, I had made Cisco a cute vest that said "Help my brothers and sisters! Donate today!" and he did his begging trick whenever someone walked by. We almost always raised more money than anyone else, and there was no way I was leaving him behind. So, even though it was far from ideal, it appeared I had no choice but to take Cisco with me when I went to deliver Cameo to her legitimate, if undeserving, owner.

I made the change in record time from my sweaty Dog Daze clothes into khaki shorts and a button-down sleeveless shirt more appropriate to a dog show judge and Humane Society volunteer. I was taking no chances with my purse today, so I tucked my phone, driver's license, and cash, along with a few waste-pickup bags, into the front pocket of my shorts and securely fastened the front tab button. I dug back into my purse for my keys and yelped when something sharp pricked my finger. I peered into the bag and saw a small gold post poking out through the lining of my purse. I probed around it and discovered an irregular shape that I knew could only be one thing.

"Oh, no," I groaned softly.

I unzipped the pocket—the same pocket in which I used to keep dog treats—and discovered a small hole, no doubt torn by dog teeth, in the bottom. I wiggled my fingers inside it and felt around until I grasped the object and pulled it out.

I gazed in resigned dismay at the little schnauzer pin in my hand. I couldn't believe I had actually suspected Corny of stealing my purse just because the pin was missing, when it had never really been missing at all. The only person who had stolen anything was me, and the worst part was that I couldn't even apologize to Corny for it.

On the other hand, just because the little pin had not been the object of a purse-snatching did not explain how it had gotten into my house in the first place.

And if I was to get Cameo back to the campground and still arrive at the fair in time to judge the dog show, I did not have time to deal with it now. I put the schnauzer pin safely away in my silverware drawer, grabbed the leashes and my day bag filled with dog supplies, and hurried across the drive to the kennel. I left Mischief and Magic in the playroom with Pepper and Marilee, and stopped by the grooming room to tell Corny I was leaving.

After what I'd suspected him of—never mind that I hadn't actually accused him of it—I felt awkward leaving Corny in charge while I was gone. But Corny, looking up from a bearded collie covered in suds, was his usual cheerful, oblivious self. "Don't you worry, Miss Stockton, all is well! I'll have Bongo here ready to go in another hour, and after that I'll have plenty of time to help with the day care dogs. Piece of cake!"

Knowing that I would be gone most of the day today, I'd made a point of not scheduling any check-ins or pickups, and only Bongo for grooming. I'd even kept the day care load light, so I didn't see what could possibly go wrong. I'd only be gone for the afternoon, and Marilee was here.

I smiled at Corny apologetically, even though of course he had no idea what I was apologizing for. "Thanks, Corny. I'll be back before closing."

"Not a problem," he assured me. "None at all!" He started to turn back to scrubbing Bongo, and then looked at me quizzically. "Miss Stockton," he said, "I know I've only been here a couple of days, but I couldn't help noticing … well, you don't really have time to run a boarding and grooming kennel, do you?"

I sighed. "The same thing has occurred to me, Corny." I glanced at my watch, and realized I also didn't have time to talk about it. "I have to run. Thanks again."

CHAPTER TWELVE

Cisco sat up straight in the backseat and panted with excitement as I turned onto the road that led to the ranger station. Back when I used to work there he came to work with me every day, and dogs have amazingly long memories for things that give them joy. Cameo, tethered in her seat belt across from him, was her usual ladylike self, resting all four paws on the bench seat while the air-conditioning vent gently ruffled her fur. There couldn't have been two more opposite dogs. I was going to miss her almost as much as Cisco was.

Since I was only going to be gone a minute, I left the car running with the air-conditioning on and dashed inside the ranger station, where the master list of all campground registrants was kept. It was a quaint, cramped little building made to resemble a rustic log cabin, with just enough room for the counter and desk, a postcard display, and a few shelves stocked with tee shirts, kitschy mugs, and colorful books about the Smokies. It always smelled like fresh cut timber and the great outdoors; even today, with the air-conditioning unit going full blast in the window.

Rick was on the phone behind the counter when I came in and he lifted his hand to me. I waved back absently, but my attention was on the camping gear stacked in a corner just inside the door. The red, white, and blue striped duffle bag was too distinctive to be missed.

"Come to volunteer?" Rick greeted me when he hung up. "We pay in peanuts and coffee, but I sure could use somebody to answer this phone while I do my job."

"Sorry," I said. "I already have one job I'm too busy for. I just need to know which campsite Tony Madison is registered in. He asked me to bring his dog."

Rick shook his head regretfully as he turned to the computer. "I heard she didn't make it."

"Yeah."

"Well, we knew it was a long shot. Still, I hate it. The police have been in and out of here since yesterday."

I nodded my head toward the camping equipment in the corner. "What's the deal?"

"Oh, you know." He picked up a pencil to jot down the site number for me. "Some homeless dude paying by the day couldn't make his campsite fee. Generally I'll cut them some slack, but we're full up."

I looked again at the red, white, and blue duffle bag. "Do you happen to know who he is?"

"Yeah, he'd be a hard one to forget. Funny-looking kid, red hair, odd name. Sounded like a college professor or something."

"Cornelius," I said, a little hollowly. "Cornelius Lancaster the Third."

"That's it." He held out the sticky note with Tony Madison's site number on it. "Do you know him?"

"Yeah." I took the note. "He checked in Friday, right?" Because by the time he could have gotten here on Thursday night, the campgrounds would have been closed. I wondered where he had spent the night Thursday. And then I thought I knew.

Rick scratched his head. "Nah, it was earlier in the week. Monday or Tuesday, seems like. He paid for a couple of days, then ran out of cash I guess and packed up on Thursday. He was back here bright and early Friday morning, though, before I even opened the gates. Good thing too, because I gave him the last tent spot. Nice enough fellow. Rides a bike everywhere he goes. No law against that, I guess. Paid in cash for Friday, then said he was getting a paycheck and could I please hold the site for him. I told him I couldn't promise. Anyhow, I guess it didn't work out, because it looks like that one-day fee was all he had."

Of course it was. Out of the ten-dollar tip I'd given him, he'd spent seven dollars for the campsite, three dollars for farm-stand blueberry muffins, and his employer hadn't paid him yet. I felt awful.

I said, reaching into my pocket, "How about if I pay for the site? Could you—"

But he held up his hand. "Like I said, I'd like to, but it's already rented. There's not a single spot left on this whole mountain this weekend."

I let my hand drop. "Well, could you at least let me take him his stuff?"

"I'm not supposed to, but ..." He shrugged. "The rules say if it's not picked up by noon we send it on to Goodwill. Seeing as it's you, go ahead, if you think you can find him."

"Oh, I can find him, all right." I picked up the duffle bag and the compact tent bag just as the phone rang. "Thanks, Rick."

He waved at me and picked up the phone. I heard him say, "Ranger Station," as I pushed through the door.

A lot of the pieces were beginning to fall into place, but the gaps that were still left formed a very confusing picture. This explained why Corny hadn't wanted to fill out the employment papers: he didn't have an address to list. And it explained what he had been doing here on the night he'd seen April and Cameo get into the car with Tony Madison. But it did not explain why a college student from an upscale place like Chapel Hill—with or without a trust fund—would be unable to pay a $7.00 campsite rental, even if he did prefer a bicycle to a car. All kids had credit cards these days. Didn't they?

Before I left the ranger station, I took out my phone and scrolled down until I found the number of Professor Rudolph. I dialed and sat in the parking lot waiting for him to answer. I was surprised when he actually did.

I told him who I was, and reminded him why I was calling. He was quick to remember. "Yes, yes," he assured me. "I was so sorry not to connect with you earlier, but of course I want to do whatever I can to help young Cornelius out. A fine young man, none better. I'm so glad to hear he landed on his feet. What can I answer for you?"

I said, "You were one of his professors at Duke?"

There was a short silence. "Why, no. I do teach at Duke University, but as far as I know Cornelius was never enrolled there. He worked for me—odd jobs, dog walking, some yard work, that sort of thing. Most industrious young fellow I've ever known, and he was a magician with Sophie, my Great Dane. Of course we talked about getting him into a program at Duke, and even looked into some scholarships. He is a brilliant young man, tested very high in math and science. I believe he took some courses at the junior college but frankly, even with a scholarship, the university was far beyond his means, and that was before the tragedy."

I put in quickly, "The tragedy?"

"He lost both his parents in a fire on Christmas Eve last year. It was a terrible blow, as I'm sure you can imagine. There was no insurance, I'm sorry to say, and barely enough money for the funeral. Afterwards, Cornelius just disappeared. I've thought about him often, wondered what became of him."

I said, with some difficulty, "So there's no trust fund?"

"What?"

"Nothing," I said quickly. "Never mind. Thank you, Professor."

"He's working with animals, did you say?" said the professor. "Excellent. You won't be disappointed, I promise you that. A very industrious young man."

I thanked the professor again and hung up. I drove to the Bottleneck Campground with confusion and uncertainty nagging at me like a toothache.

The RV sites at Bottleneck were nice enough, but too narrow and close together for my taste. Each site was shaded, though, and most of them were within hearing range of the tumbling waters—when their generators weren't roaring, of course. I found site #21 and parked in the shade, rolling down all the windows for the dogs. The RV looked empty, the campsite deserted. In the site to the right a woman was hanging wet swimsuits on the line, and in the camp to the left four adults were gathered around a camp table, chatting and sipping coffee. I walked around the side of the Madisons' RV and knocked. "Hello," I called when there was no sign of movement inside. I knocked again. "Hello, Mr. Madison, I've brought your dog!"

I walked all the way around the vehicle, standing on tiptoe to try to see inside the darkened windows. I noticed a tow hitch on the back, but no car. I could only guess he had been on his way back from Asheville when I'd talked to him on the phone, and had been delayed. I went back to the door and knocked one more time.

The woman who was hanging up swimsuits finally took pity on me and called, "Honey, he's not there."

I walked over to her. "I've been keeping his dog for him," I explained. "He asked me to bring her by this morning."

She shrugged. "He peeled out of here about forty-five minutes ago," she said. "Seemed in an awful hurry. There are speed limits on these roads, you know. People walking, kids playing. Somebody ought to get out and enforce the law, if you ask me."

I began, "Well, the forest service doesn't really have the ..." And then I broke off, frowning. "Forty-five minutes, you say?"

"More or less."

That would've been right after he talked to me. Why would he leave when he knew I was on my way?

"Do you want me to tell him you were here?" the woman volunteered.

"Thanks, I'll wait a little longer," I said. "Maybe he just had to run out and get something. He knew I was coming."

I turned to go back to the car and sit with the dogs when a plume of dust approaching us on the road caught my eye. The vehicle was going pretty fast, and from the way the lady next door had just described Tony Madison's departure, I thought it might be him returning. But only for a moment. I stepped back out of the way as the sheriff's department's K-9 unit pulled up in front of the campsite, followed closely by a patrol car.

Jolene got out of the SUV, glaring at me. I heard the two doors of the patrol car slam and Deke and Mike approached, their hands close to their gun belts. The formerly friendly woman next door looked at me warily and took a step back; the people in the site on the other side got up from the table and moved closer, craning to see what was happening.

"Stockton," Jolene said curtly, "what are you doing here?"

I lifted my hands in mock surrender. "Hey, I'm just doing my job. Mr. Madison told me to return his dog. But he's not here. That lady," I nodded toward the woman next door, "said he left forty-five minutes ago."

Jolene looked at Deke and jerked her head toward the RV. They immediately moved forward, Deke banging on the door, Mike moving around the opposite side. I heard Deke call, "Tony Madison, this is the Hanover County Sheriff's Department. We have a warrant for your arrest. Please open the door now or we will break it down. Mr. Madison!"

I swung my gaze back to Jolene. "Warrant?"

She said, "Return to your vehicle. Stay out of the way. Do not leave the premises."

She strode up to the RV and I heard her say to Deke, "Break it down."

Let the record show that up to this point I'd been more than cooperative with the police. But I was getting a little tired of Deputy Jolene telling me where to go, when to go, and what to do when I got there, especially since, in this instance, I knew perfectly well there was no one inside that RV and the chances of gunplay were pretty slim. So while the onlookers shrank back with wide eyes when the officers drew their guns and Deke kicked open the flimsy lock on the RV, I walked over to the lady with the swimsuits.

"My name is Raine," I said. I gestured toward my car, where Cisco was watching the proceedings with interest from his open window; Cameo rested her chin on the other window and didn't seem very impressed at all. "The white golden retriever is Mr. Madison's, and that's my dog Cisco on the other side. Do you remember what kind of car Mr. Madison was driving?"

She looked at me suspiciously. "Are you with the police?"

"No," I admitted. "But—"

"Then I shouldn't be talking to you." Immediately contradicting herself, she added anxiously, "What's going on? What are they arresting him for? It's not drugs, is it? Because I've got kids. Good heavens, in a national forest campground, there should be a law."

I heard Deke shout, "Clear!" and Mike echoed, "Clear!" It was an RV, after all. There weren't that many places to hide.

I said, "There is a law. That is, there are lots of laws, and that's why people get arrested when they break them. It would really help me out if you could tell me what kind of car he was driving. Even the color."

"You planning to chase him down, Stockton?" Jolene came up behind me, scowling as usual. "I thought I told you to stay out of the way."

"I am out of the way," I returned sweetly. "I'm all the way over here, talking to this nice lady, who saw Tony Madison drive away this morning. If I knew what kind of car he was driving, I could give you even more information."

Jolene turned to the other woman. "Is that right, ma'am?"

She nodded, looking more self-important than alarmed now. "That's right. He looked to be in a big hurry, too."

"What time was that?"

"Like I told her ..." she indicated me. "It was about forty-five minutes before you all got here."

"That would be," I added helpfully, "right after I told him his wife's ex-husband was in town."

Jolene turned to look at me, her features inscrutable. Then she raised her hand to Mike and said, "Mike, will you come take this lady's statement, please? Deke, see if the people on the other side know anything."

She took out her notebook and gestured me back toward the Madison campsite. "Talk to me, Stockton."

"The ex-husband's name is Greg Sellers," I said. "He's a private investigator from Virginia. I think he's the one who planted the transmitter in Cameo's collar and he's probably the one who stole my purse."

She looked up from jotting notes, her eyes like stone. "You knew we were investigating this as a possible homicide, and you didn't mention to us that there was an ex-husband involved?"

"I just found out myself an hour ago," I returned impatiently. "As I was saying—"

"So naturally your first call is to the murder suspect."

That gave me pause. I admitted uncomfortably, "I didn't think of that."

"Which is exactly why we're the police and you're not," she returned sharply. "Do you know I could charge you with obstruction of justice right now?"

"No," I replied, just as sharply. "You could have an hour ago, but right now I'm trying my best to tell you everything I know if you'd just be quiet and listen."

Her nostrils flared and I'm sure if there had been a law against telling an officer to be quiet, she would have slapped the cuffs on me that minute. Instead she demanded, "What makes you think he planted the transmitter?"

"I saw him trying to break into my car on Friday. Cameo's collar was on the front seat. A friend of mine traced the plate, that's how I know his name. But," I assured her hastily, "I only got the information this morning."

She shot me a dagger look and I volunteered, "Marshall Becker." She wrote it down.

I went on, "That night someone tried to break into my kennel. The collar was in my office. He was driving the same kind of car as Sellers. The thing is …" Now I frowned, thinking it through as I spoke. "All this time I've been thinking it was Tony Madison who planted the transmitter in Cameo's collar to spy on his wife. But he never showed the least bit of interest in getting Cameo, or the collar, back. I don't think he knew the device was there. When I told Mr. Madison that Sellers was in town, he seemed shocked, and right after that he took off. Unless he somehow found out you were on the way to arrest him …" I looked questioningly at her, and she shook her head.

"We just got the warrant this morning. The blood on the post at the overlook was a match, and yesterday we got a warrant to search the RV and found a blood-smeared paper towel in the trash, like someone had used it to wipe their hands. It matched April Madison's too. He said something about her cutting herself in the kitchen, but he knew we had the evidence. If he was going to run, it would have been last night." Now her expression grew thoughtful. "No, it was something about you mentioning Sellers."

"Could Sellers be a witness?" I suggested.

"Maybe." She added, "You don't happen to know where Sellers is staying, do you?"

"No, but Marshall has his tag number. His cell phone number, too." In the interest of full disclosure, I added, "I left a message for Greg Sellers to call me back. If I talk to him I can—"

"You can do nothing," she interrupted harshly. "Listen to me, Stockton. Stay away from both of those men, and if either of them attempts to contact you call the police immediately. Do you understand?"

I said, "Do you think Sellers is involved in the murder?"

"He is now," she said grimly. "He's in possession of what may be material evidence in our case and he's probably being stalked by our prime suspect. At the very least, he's in danger, which makes him a dangerous man to be around. Our job is to find him before Marshall does." She pulled out her phone. "Your job is to go back to ..." She made a vague gesture with her free hand. "Doing whatever it is you do."

I drew a breath for a retort, but she spoke into the phone. "Track down Marshall Becker and patch him through to me on this line. It's urgent. And put me through to the sheriff."

She glanced at me and moved the phone away from her mouth. "By the way, Madison drives a white

CR-V. Did you really think we wouldn't already have a BOLO out on it?"

I returned sourly, "You'll find Marshall Becker at the county fair. He's judging jams."

I turned on my heel to go as she said into the phone, "Sheriff, there's been a development."

CHAPTER THIRTEEN

When I'd mapped out my plan for the morning, I had not included the time it would take to be interviewed by the police. I also had intended to be leaving the campground with one less dog than I'd started with, and while the unexpected turn of events might have suited Cisco just fine, it left me in something of a dilemma. I could either go home and drop off Cameo, or get to the fair in time to keep my commitment to judge the dog show. There were thirteen anxious young men and women with their spiffed-up dogs waiting for me, so there really wasn't much of a choice.

Of course, when I'd volunteered months ago to do back-to-back duty at the fair, I'd thought Miles and Melanie would be with me. Melanie would have proudly held Cisco's leash while I judged the dog show and would have been the perfect little carnival barker at the Humane Society booth, urging people to come on over while shaking the donation jar in their faces, probably charging them a dollar each to take a picture with Cisco. Miles would have carried our gear and brought us cold drinks and his eyes would have twinkled a lot. The stab of loss and regret I felt was so intense it hurt my stomach.

I parked again in the back lot and dragged my lightweight canvas crate—lightweight being a relative term—out of the back of the SUV, along with the day bag that contained Cisco's vest, water, treats, and other doggie necessities, as well as a roll of duct tape for securing posters at the booth and colored markers for the signs. One crate for two big dogs was bound to be an adventure, but at least they liked each other. Besides, I had no choice.

Lugging the crate, bag, and the two golden retrievers across the dusty field, I was left red-faced and dripping sweat in no time. My knee was starting to ache, and I had to move slowly to favor it. I also have to say my mood wasn't the best, and with every ounce of my concentration focused on keeping Cisco and Cameo under control as we approached the noise and crowds of the midway, I jumped a little when a dry voice said next to me, "Thanks for the heads-up about the police, Miss Stockton."

Marshall Becker fell into step beside me, reaching to take the heavy crate from my grip. I certainly didn't fight him for it. "If I had known there was an ongoing investigation, I never would have gotten involved," he added. "I certainly wouldn't have given the information to a private citizen."

"Sounds like something you should tell the police."

"I did. For almost an hour."

I blotted my forehead with the back of my arm, squinting in the sun. "Sorry to throw your schedule off, but I never asked you to get involved. Besides, I didn't know Greg Sellers had anything to do with the investigation until today."

He said, "What exactly do you think he has to do with it?"

"Sorry, I can't give that information to a private citizen," I replied, and he chuckled.

He said, "What happened to your knee?"

"I fell."

"Small wonder, carrying all this stuff around with two big dogs. Don't you have any help?"

Once again, I was reminded of Miles and Melanie and how everything was supposed to be different, but I refused to let the melancholy take hold. I replied instead, glancing at him, "Now I do."

He grinned, and I gestured to the big tent across the way from which the sound of barking could be heard even over the blare of midway music. "I guess we're over there. Thanks for your help."

"Not a problem. Beautiful dogs. That's an English Cream golden retriever, isn't it?"

I looked at him in surprise. "Not many people know that."

He said, "I've always had goldens. My last one, Buddy, just died last year. He was fourteen."

He rose several notches in my esteem. I said, with genuine sympathy, "I'm so sorry. It must have been hard to lose him, so soon after your wife."

He replied simply, "It was."

We arrived at the entrance to the tent and I extended my hand for the crate. "Well, this is it. Thanks again."

"I'll help you set up."

Again, that was not an offer I was about to refuse.

I could see the dismay on some of the kids' faces when I passed by with my two beautiful goldens, and the relief when they realized I was the judge, not a competitor. We were greeted by the coordinator of the local 4-H program, who quickly pinned a judge's badge on my shirt and spread out the first, second, and third place ribbons on the folding table at the front of the tent. Marshall set up the crate behind the table and I poured water into a collapsible bowl for the dogs. They each had a few laps, and I escorted them—pushed, might be a more accurate word—into the crate. There was a portable fan set up behind the judge's table, presumably for my comfort, but I turned it on the dogs.

"Okay," I said, glancing out over the lineup of dogs and the family and friends who were beginning to fill the folding chairs inside the tent. "I guess this is it." And, because I was feeling more kindly disposed toward him now that I knew he was a golden retriever person, I added, "I'm sorry I got you in trouble with Jolene. Deputy Smith, I mean. And I appreciate the help with the crate."

"That's okay," he replied. "You can make it up to me by letting me buy you that corn dog after the show."

"Look," I said, "you don't have to keep being nice to me. You already have my vote."

"Good to hear," he replied with an appreciative nod of his head, "because it would be a lot harder to persuade you to work on my campaign if you were voting for the other guy."

I gave a disbelieving shake of my head. "You really don't know when to stop, do you?"

"That's how you win elections," he assured me.

"Well, you're going to have to win this one by yourself. I'm not working on anybody's campaign. But," I added, "I will take that corn dog."

He was laughing as he walked away.

I am not a qualified dog show judge, but that's okay because this wasn't a qualified dog show. It was mostly a way to reward outstanding participants in the 4-H club's dog program and to encourage others to join, so I made sure I had something nice to say about every dog. Since most of the dogs were mixed breeds, there was no real standard: I judged on cleanliness and general grooming, manners and disposition, and basic obedience commands. The winner, hands down, was an Aussie/border collie mix, but you just can't get any smarter than that, with second place going to what looked to be a cross between a German Shepherd and a collie, and third place taken by a funny little bulldog named Gus who, I was happy to see, had not forgotten *all* of the obedience skills he had learned in puppy class at Dog Daze.

I lingered to congratulate the winners and encourage the also-rans, taking the opportunity to pass out Dog Daze business cards to moms and dads while I was there. I brought Cisco out of his crate and let him do a few tricks for a dog biscuit, and one of the parents was nice enough to hold his leash while I got Cameo out and folded up the crate. Of course there were a lot of oohs and ahhs over Cameo, who really was a striking-looking dog, and she preened under the attention.

I dragged my camp down the midway to the Humane Society booth, which was decorated with colorful dog and cat flags and paw print bunting, and was once again flushed and sweating by the time I got there—not to mention hungry. I was beginning to hope Marshall had been serious about that corn dog. I wondered where he had gone off to until I heard, muffled by distance and carousel music, a microphoned voice saying something about the land of the free and the home of the brave, followed by cheers and applause. His speech. Of course.

The volunteer I relieved helped me set up the crate and get the dogs situated before she left. I put Cameo in the crate with a bowl of water and a chew toy, and let Cisco, wearing his "Donate now!" vest, sit beside me at the table that held brochures, volunteer signup sheets, and the donation jar.

With two show-stoppers like Cisco and Cameo, I would have been foolish not to take advantage of both of them, and I planned to take turns letting them wear the vest and work the crowd. Cisco and I did a brisk business, although I will admit, most of the people who stopped by just wanted to pet Cisco and tell me about their own dogs, dropping only a handful of change into the jar when they left. But quarters and nickels are better than nothing at all, and I actually like hearing about other peoples' dogs.

Midway through my shift I switched out the dogs, zipping Cisco into the crate and slipping the "Donate" vest over Cameo's head. She seemed pretty sanguine about the whole thing, and Cisco was happy as long as he could see her—and enjoy his chew bone, of course. I had no reason to expect trouble, so I was completely caught off guard when Cameo suddenly gave a series of joyful barks and leapt forward, jerking the leash out of my hand as she plunged into the crowd.

I cried, "Cameo!"

Panic surged as I rushed after her. A dog loose in this crowd might never be seen again, especially one as pretty as Cameo, and if I lost her for the second time ... But I only had to run a few steps before my fears were allayed. A fairgoer had caught her—or perhaps it would be more accurate to say she had caught him. She was standing with her front paws on his chest, grinning, while he ruffled her fur and scratched her ears and exclaimed, "Hey, there, pretty girl! Aren't you looking fine?"

I said, gasping, "I'm so sorry! She got away from me." I reached for the leash and then caught my breath as the man looked up at me. It was the same balding, stoop-shouldered tourist who'd tried to break into my car ... only he wasn't stoop-shouldered now, and he didn't look like a tourist.

He was wearing neat khaki pants and a short-sleeved, buttoned white shirt, and he moved with confidence and assurance. He said, "Cameo, off."

Cameo obeyed him, four feet on the ground, looking up at him adoringly. He smiled as he extended his hand to me. "Miss Stockton," he said. "I'm Greg Sellers."

I extended my hand too; not to shake his but to snatch Cameo's leash. "Mr. Sellers," I said, "you should know the police are looking for you."

"I'm not surprised." A shadow of pain came over his face as he added, "I heard about April. I'm sure they want to interview me. I was on my way to the sheriff's department when I got your call. I thought it would save time all around if I could bring them some information they could actually use."

I looked at him warily. "How did you find me?"

"You said you were working a booth at the fair. I'm a detective. I figured it out." Again he smiled. "Also, I saw Cameo across the midway."

If I could get past the fact that he had tried to break into my car and my kennel, had snatched my purse and kicked my feet out from under me in the process, I might have been fooled into thinking he was a pleasant man. Even nice. I was having almost as much of a hard time reconciling his demeanor with his behavior as I was trying to believe that this well-dressed, well-spoken man was the same bumbling tourist I'd met only two days ago.

I could hear Cisco barking anxiously, and I knew if I didn't return soon he would break right through the zippered mesh door of the crate. It wasn't as though he'd never done it before. I glanced uneasily over my shoulder, back toward my booth. "I have to get back."

He walked with me the few dozen steps back toward the colorful Humane Society booth. Cameo trotted between us happily, her head up tilted to keep her eyes on Sellers, her golden retriever smile lighting up her whole face. I said, "Cameo seems to like you."

He flashed a grin down at Cameo. "Yeah, she's my bud. I've had her since she was eight weeks old. After the divorce, I insisted on visitation rights. Of course ..." And the grin faded. "Once April married Madison, that wasn't so easy anymore."

I remembered Tony Madison saying when Jolene interviewed him in the hospital, "None of this would have happened except for that damn dog." I'd thought he meant that if April hadn't gone out searching for a lost dog she never would have fallen. But now the police had evidence that she hadn't fallen, at least by accident. Was it possible that what had begun as a custody dispute over a dog had ended in murder?

I drew Cameo closer to me as we reached the booth. Cisco was standing in his crate, nose pressed to the mesh door, tail wagging madly. I moved behind the table, folding another loop in the leash to keep Cameo close, and said boldly, "I guess that explains how you were able to plant the transmitter in her collar."

To my surprise, he didn't deny it. "Madison was trying to convince April to move to California. That's what this trip was about, or at least that's what he claimed." His brows drew together in a way that seemed fierce to me, but it might have simply been in an effort to hide his grief. "I was afraid he was planning something like this, and it turns out I was right. I couldn't let her go off alone with him, so I put the transmitter in Cameo's collar to keep up with them."

I thought that anyone who would use an electronic bug to spy on his ex-wife and her new husband—not to mention tracking them across the country—was a little sick, but sometimes I actually do think before I speak, so I said nothing. Besides, at that moment a little boy dragged his parents over to the booth, eagerly pointing at Cameo, and demanded, "Does your dog bite?"

"All dogs bite," I told him, and tried to soften my words with a smile. I'm not sure how well I did, since most of my attention was still on the man next to me. "What you want to do is make sure they don't bite you."

I went into an abbreviated version of my lecture on dog safety, showed him how to scratch Cameo under the chin instead of coming over her head with an open hand, and handed the parents a brochure. They let the kid put a dollar into the donation jar.

I said, when they were gone, "What I don't understand is why you didn't try to find April when she first went missing. If you were listening to everything that was going on you must have known something was wrong."

"You have to be within a few hundred yards to pick up a voice transmission," he explained, "that's why the device is equipped with a recorder. I lost the GPS signal on Tuesday night and I did know something was wrong, but there was nothing I could do about it. I didn't know where they were."

I said, "Cameo was with April, in the gorge."

He nodded, "That's why I couldn't get a signal until she was picked up on Thursday morning. I tracked her—or at least her collar—to town, and to the vet's, and to your place."

I said, "Why didn't you just come up and introduce yourself, instead of following me and trying to break into my kennel?"

He shook his head with an expression that was part sad, part rueful. "And say what? That I had planted an electronic bug in the dog's collar to stalk my ex-wife? Would you really have turned Cameo over to me under those circumstances? You would have called the police and I wouldn't have been able to do anything."

He was right about that.

"Besides," he went on, "I still didn't know what had happened to April. As far as I knew Madison might have dumped Cameo and taken off with her. I knew Cameo was safe with you. Finding April was my first priority."

Another family came up, admired Cameo, and dropped some coins into the jar. I smiled and thanked them, but forgot to give them a brochure. I turned back to Sellers. "Look," I said, not particularly graciously, "I know you think you did the right thing, and who knows? Maybe it'll turn out you did. But the truth of the matter is that you were stalking your ex-wife and that's not going to put you in a very good light in the eyes of the police. The best thing you can do is turn yourself in."

His lips tightened, causing grim brackets to appear at either side of his mouth. "I stalked my ex-wife," he said, putting emphasis on the word "stalked," "because she married a killer. Tony Madison has been married three times before, and each wife has died less than a year after they were married. They all had life insurance policies. Fifty thousand, seventy-five … nothing outrageous, but I guess it's worth killing for. He lives off of the insurance until it runs out and then he marries somebody else. April had a hundred-fifty-thousand-dollar policy from her job."

I stared at him. "But if that's true, the police …"

"There was an investigation after the last wife," Sellers said. "Of course they weren't able to pin anything on him. He'd had two to practice on by then, and they all were made to look like accidents. Just like April's accident."

My thoughts were spinning. How could the guy make something like that up? And if Tony Madison had killed four wives, including April, it certainly explained why he had run when I'd mentioned Greg Sellers was tracking him. I said, "You need to take this to the police."

He replied patiently, "That's exactly what I intend to do. But it won't mean anything unless I can also take them the proof."

He looked as though he expected me to say something, and when I didn't, he prompted, "Don't you see? The device *records*. If Cameo was with April when Madison knocked her out and threw her into the gorge, and I'm almost certain she was, then everything that happened in those last minutes is recorded on that chip. That's why I need it before I go to the police."

I looked at him blankly. "What? But—you already have it. You stole it out of my purse last night!"

Now it was he who looked confused. "Stole it? What are you talking about?"

"Are you telling me you didn't follow me to the fair last night?" I demanded angrily. "Because I know it was you! It had to be!"

His expression was caution mixed with reluctance. "All right," he admitted. "I followed you here. But it's not like the thing is a beacon, you know. I knew you were somewhere on the fairgrounds, but I was never able to find you. It was almost dark, and I might've walked right past you without recognizing you."

And he might well have done so, when Cameo caught the scent of someone in the crowd and burst into the same kind of happy barking she'd demonstrated when she pulled the leash out of my hands a few minutes ago. Sonny had said it was her dad. Foolishly, I'd thought she meant Tony Madison.

"But," I said, floundering, "someone knocked me down, stole my purse. And the only thing they took from it was the transmitter."

Greg Sellers looked at me in confusion and dismay. "Miss Stockton," he said, "I checked the GPS on that device half an hour ago, and it clearly shows it's still at your address."

CHAPTER FOURTEEN

All I could think was, *Corny*. It had been Corny after all. I didn't know how, or why, but what other explanation could there be? He had shown up almost at the same time as Cameo, hadn't he? He had known every detail of my schedule for the past two days. He had even been staying at the same campground as April Madison. And if the transmitter was tracking to my address now, he was the only one who was there. Even Marilee only worked half days on Saturdays and was long gone. It *had* to be him.

But I just couldn't believe it.

I said slowly, "I think I know who has it."

There was a quickening of expectation in his eyes. "Can you get it back?"

"I don't know." I bit down on my thumbnail anxiously. "I could be wrong."

A group of teenagers stopped by the table, picked up some brochures and put them down again, nudged each other, and pointed to Cameo. "Hey," said one of them, "is that dog for sale?"

I said, "No." And hoped the brief answer would send them on their way.

Another one said, "Last year at the fair they were giving away puppies."

I said, "The humane society doesn't give away puppies. If you want to adopt a dog you have to fill out a form and be approved. The cost is sixty dollars."

One of them guffawed. "For a *dog*?"

I bit down on my impatience. "The fee includes spay or neuter surgery and all shots. And," I added pointedly, "you have to be twenty-one or older to apply."

The group wandered off, looking disgruntled, and Sellers said, "I don't mean to be pushy, Miss Stockton, but the longer I delay going to the police with my information, the less likely I am to be believed—unless I have evidence, of course. I've got to get that transmitter back."

I said, "You need to tell the police what you know. I'll look again for the transmitter, and if I find it I'll turn it in. That's all I can do."

There was a moment, just a moment, when I thought he might object, but then he nodded. "Fair enough. You have my cell number." He started to turn away.

I said, "How did you know she'd been hit over the head?"

He looked back at me, puzzled.

"I mean, until this morning everyone, including the police, thought April had fallen."

He smiled, understanding. "I have a police scanner in my car."

I said, "Oh," and tried to smile back. I probably wasn't very convincing.

He said soberly, "This is important, Miss Stockton. What's recorded on that device may be the only way we can stop a serial killer."

"I know," I said. "I'll find it."

He nodded and walked away. Cameo whined and tugged at the leash as she watched him go.

I glanced at my watch. I still had another half hour before the end of my shift, and that seemed like far too long. Before I could decide what to do, I was besieged by another group of fairgoers, this one complete with three small children holding sticks of cotton candy. Cisco stood up in his crate and barked when he saw the cotton candy, and one of the toddlers, startled, dropped his candy on Cameo's head. The toddler wailed, his siblings laughed, and the parents frantically tried to herd the group away while I scrubbed at Cameo's sticky ears with a tissue dipped in the dogs' water dish.

"Looks like you've got your hands full," said a male voice behind me, "again."

I glanced over my shoulder to see Marshall Becker place a red and white box filled with concession stand food on the table. "Do you have time for a lunch break?" he asked.

"I, um ..." I straightened up, distracted, and glanced at the food. "Thank you, that's nice. Could you do me a favor?" I thrust Cameo's leash into his hand. "Hold her for a minute. I have to make a phone call."

Without waiting for a reply I dug my phone out of my pocket and walked away from the crowd as I dialed. Jolene answered on the second ring.

"Okay," I said, before she could say something to make me mad, "you told me to call if I saw Greg Sellers so I'm calling. He was here only a few minutes ago, at my booth at the fair. The thing is, I don't think he's the one who stole my purse anymore. He was looking for the transmitter. He thinks I still have it."

Jolene said tersely, "Is he still there?"

I covered my free ear with my hand to block out some of the noise and music. "No. He wants to meet me later."

"How long ago did you see him?"

"I don't know. Five, six minutes."

I heard her muffle the mouthpiece with her hand and speak to someone, but I couldn't hear what she was saying. It went on longer than I liked and I said, just a little sarcastically, "Hey, sorry to bother you. You told me to call."

She came back on the line. "Stockton, listen to me. I'm here at a homicide scene. Tony Madison's CR-V was found a few minutes ago behind the abandoned furniture warehouse on Highway 83. Madison's body was inside, shot through the chest."

I managed on a single indrawn breath, "And you think Sellers ...?"

"He is a person of very particular interest in this case, yes. Under no circumstances are you to meet with Sellers again. We have a team at the fair now and the sheriff is dispatching two more units. If Sellers is still at the fairgrounds, we'll find him. Meanwhile, you need to stay away from him."

My heart was thumping unevenly. Tony Madison, dead. But how could he be? He was the one who had killed April. He had killed three other wives and had fled when he heard the name of Greg Sellers, who knew the truth. Why was he dead?

I said, "Jolene, you didn't say anything on the police band about April being knocked out before she went into the gorge, did you?"

"What?" Her tone was sharp. "We never discuss details of an investigation on the radio. That's what our phones are for. Why do you ask that?"

I swallowed hard. "He knows where I live. Sellers. And he thinks the transmitter is at my house."

There was the briefest of pauses. "We'll dispatch a unit to your house. You stay put."

"My dogs are there!"

But she had already hung up. "Damn it," I whispered. I stared at the phone, not knowing what to do. What if Sellers got there before the deputies did? I wanted to call Corny and warn him, but what would I say? If Corny did know where the transmitter was, he would only take it and run. If he didn't, what could he do that the police could not?

One thing was certain. I could not stay here while the man who had probably murdered Tony Madison was on his way to my house.

Marshall was using a handful of paper napkins to sponge the cotton candy off of Cameo's fur when I returned to the booth, and was doing a much better job than I had done. Cisco stood in his crate, watching intently. I wasn't sure whether he was jealous of the attention or worried about competition for Cameo's affection.

Marshall glanced up from telling Cameo what a beautiful girl she was, and his smile faded a little when he saw me. "Is everything okay?"

"Um, actually, no." I glanced around worriedly. "I have to get home. Something's come up. Listen, I hate to ask, but ..." I looked at him apologetically. "My shift isn't over for half an hour and I can't leave the booth unmanned ... is there any way you could sit here and keep an eye on the donation jar until my relief gets here?"

He lifted an eyebrow, looking amused as he straightened up. "That's a pretty big favor."

"This is one of the most popular booths at the fair," I pointed out, reaching for Cameo's leash. "And people always vote for animal lovers."

"How are people going to know I'm an animal lover if you take the dog?"

I was getting a little frantic. Every minute I stayed here was another minute Mischief, Magic, and Pepper—not to mention all the other dogs in the kennel—were vulnerable. And it wasn't just paranoia. Once a crazy man had set my kennel on fire. Another one had thrown a Molotov cocktail, and yet another had tried to drive his truck through the front of my house. I knew what could happen, and I could not stay here, oblivious, while it did.

I slung the day bag over my shoulder and said quickly, "I'll take Cameo to the car and be right back for Cisco and the crate. All you have to do is sit here and make sure no one walks off with the donation jar. Thank you so much!"

He replied, "You owe me."

I waved an acknowledgement and hurried off with Cameo, Cisco barking indignantly after us. I called over my shoulder, "Cisco! Quiet!" But apparently he didn't hear me. His increasingly anxious barking followed me down the midway, and although I'd like to think he was barking for me, I knew it was all about Cameo.

I took the shortcut behind the carousel to the employee parking lot, hurrying Cameo along despite my throbbing knee. This time of day the entire back of the fairgrounds was relatively deserted, which was not that surprising since most of the entertainment and special events would take place after dark. The silver equipment trailers at the other side of the field practically shimmered in the heat, and a still dusty haze hung over the parking lot. Even the woods looked dry and wilted, and my footsteps crunched on the hard-packed dirt as I hurried across the lot. I dug into my pocket for my keys, and that's when Greg Sellers fell into step beside me.

Cameo began panting excitedly and tried to lunge across my body to get to him, almost tripping me. I pulled her back instinctively and stopped still, darting my eyes around for options.

"Just keep moving," Sellers said. He had one hand in the pocket of his trousers and he lifted it now, revealing the rubber grip of a compact, snub-nosed pistol. His voice and his smile were pleasant as he took my arm with his other hand, urging me forward. "Glad to see you were able to get away early. I thought it would be more efficient if I helped you search. I'll ride with you, if you don't mind. I'd take my own car but the front parking lot is swarming with police. I guess you called them."

Somehow I managed, in an almost normal tone, "I thought you were going to tell them what you know."

"Well, like I explained, that's really not going to be in my best interests right now."

"Especially," I suggested, desperately trying to keep my voice even, "since the police just found Tony Madison's body."

His hand tightened on my arm. "Keep moving. Hurry up."

I pretended to stumble. "I can't walk any faster. I hurt my knee last night when you pushed me down."

He was unsympathetic. "Good thing you don't have to go very far, then."

If I could stall long enough, surely someone would come down the path, or turn into the parking lot, or one of the deputies would think to patrol the employee lot. I thought about screaming or trying to break away, but I didn't know where the gun was. I thought about letting Cameo go, but she would only trot right over to the man she adored. My phone was in my pocket, and it was absolutely useless unless I could break away long enough to call for help.

I said, "I don't understand. You had my purse, why didn't you take the transmitter?"

"Don't mess with me," he returned briefly. "If it had been in your purse, I would've found it. So now you're going to show me where you really hid it. And we don't have a lot of time."

I said, "It's not going to be Tony Madison's voice on that recorder, is it? It's yours."

His lips tightened into a thin line. "I would never hurt April. I tried to save her from that bastard. That's why I picked her up that evening when she was out walking Cameo. I had to warn her about what I'd found out about Madison, I never would have let her know I was following them if I hadn't thought it was life and death. Of course she was mad about my being here, even after I explained things to her. She wouldn't listen to me. She made me pull the car over on the other side of the mountain, by that overlook, and she and Cameo got out. It was getting dark and I didn't want to leave her there. We argued about it and she pulled out her phone to call Madison. I tried to get the phone away from her and when she walked away I grabbed Cameo and put her in the car. April started yelling at me and I was afraid somebody would hear so I let her have the dog and I drove off. But I felt bad about leaving her out there on the side of the road so I came back after about twenty minutes … Just in time to see Madison pull up by the overlook. It was nearly full dark by then, and I turned off my headlights so he wouldn't see me. She was standing by the overlook and when he drove up she turned around. He came up to her and took her by the shoulders like he was going to kiss her, then he slammed her head against the rail post hard enough to crack her skull. Cameo started barking. April slumped down and he dragged her up and over the rail and pushed her into the gorge. Then he got into his car and drove away."

We had stopped walking. His face was tight and gray with the memory, his eyes dull with the effort to repress emotion. "I got out," he finished quietly. "I ran to the rail, I looked ... but all I could see was Cameo, scrambling down into the gorge. I thought April was dead."

"Why didn't you call someone?" I said. "Why didn't you tell them what had happened? April was alive for two days in that gorge! We might have saved her!"

"Don't you think I know that?" He turned on me with his face torn with anguish. His fingers dug into my upper arm so hard that I had to smother a cry, and I shrank back from his fury. "I thought she was dead! I thought she was dead and I couldn't tell anybody because of that damn transmitter! Mine was the last voice on it—my voice arguing with her, threatening her. The recorder didn't pick up her phone call to Madison because Cameo was in the car with me when she made it. I thought April was dead and all the evidence pointed to me!"

He gave my arm a single hard shake and I lost my balance and almost fell. Cameo looked at me, and at him, anxiously. If anyone had been around to witness that, surely someone would have come to my rescue. There must have been over a thousand people at the fair today; how could none of them be in this parking lot?

He took a swift, calming breath and started walking again, pushing me forward toward the rows of cars. "I went back to look for Cameo, but by then I'd lost her signal. I didn't pick it up again for two days."

I said, "How did you find Madison today?"

"I didn't," he replied. "He found me. Called me, to be precise, after someone—I'm guessing you—told him I was here. He had some idea that I'd recorded the murder, and he tried to threaten me with some cock-and-bull story he was going to take to the police if I didn't turn over the evidence."

"So you agreed to meet him behind the warehouse," I said, "and you shot him." I could see my car at the end of the row just ahead of us. I put my thumb on the panic button of the key fob, having faint hope that it would do any good. No one even noticed car alarms anymore, and if anyone did he would simply think I had lost my car in the parking lot and was using the alarm to locate it. But it might distract Sellers long enough …

"He killed four women!" Sellers said harshly. "He deserved to die! Whoever shot him did the world a favor."

"I'm not arguing that," I told him, weighing my options, trying to stay calm. "Maybe it was even self-defense. But you'll have a better chance of the police believing your story if you go to them now. They already have a county-wide search out for you. Maybe even roadblocks." Probably not true, but he had no way of knowing that.

"They can't tie me to Madison. The only thing that ties me to anything is that damn transmitter. As soon as I have it, all our problems will be over."

My car was only a few dozen steps away. I could not let him get in my car. If he drove to my house he would see the police cruiser that had been dispatched there and I would be a kidnap victim. If by some chance the deputies had the foresight to conceal their presence, Sellers had a gun and the chances of leaving my property without shots being fired were very, very slim.

The first rule of survival: never let the criminal take you to a second location. Not ever.

I said, "I'm parked over there," and I tried to turn the opposite way. His grip steered me straight.

"Nice try, Miss Stockton," he said. "I know your car."

Suddenly Cameo turned around, tugging on the leash, and barked. My heart leapt as I heard an answering bark and I swiveled my head, crying, "Cisco!" I saw him flying toward me, ears slicked back, tongue lolling, a wild and joyful triumph in his eyes. The flimsy canvas crate with its zippered door would not hold a determined golden retriever, and this was not the first time he had broken through it in pursuit of something he loved.

I dropped Cameo's leash and the two dogs met in a playful bounce a few feet away from us, rolling over in the dirt parking lot, leashes tangling. Sellers took a half-turning step toward the ruckus, surprised enough to lighten his grip on my arm. I used the opportunity to transfer the keys to my free hand and I called, "Cisco!"

He looked up at me happily. "Cisco, fetch!"

I drew back my arm and tossed the keys as far as I could into the field of weeds. Cisco took off after them with Cameo in hot pursuit, and I took advantage of Sellers's confusion to wrench my arm away and run as fast as I could in the opposite direction.

I knew I wouldn't make it very far. But I was younger and lighter than Sellers, and, even with a bum knee, I thought I could reach the row of supply trucks and use them to hide long enough to call 911 before he caught up with me. I almost made it, too. I had my phone in hand when a sudden patch of uneven earth sent a shaft of pain through my knee and I went sprawling in the shadow of one of the silver trucks. My phone flew from my hand, the contents of my day bag scattered, and Greg Sellers dragged me to my feet by my hair. I screamed then, but no one could hear. In the background, bluegrass music wailed and children squealed on the Ferris wheel and announcers' voices boomed through the microphone. It occurred to me that if Sellers fired his pistol, people would think it was the sound of fireworks.

I struggled harder, but the man was twice my size and stronger than he looked. He grabbed my arms and twisted them behind my back, slamming me up against the side of the supply truck hard enough to knock my breath away. In a moment I heard a ripping sound and felt my wrists being bound tightly together. He had found the duct tape that had fallen from my bag and was using it to tie my hands. He growled in my ear, "You'd better hope that dog of yours finds those keys."

Cisco was a retriever, and more importantly, a search dog. It was entirely possible he would be able to find one set of keys in the vast field of tall weeds, but the point had been to get Cisco to run, not to retrieve. "He'll never bring them to you," I gasped, just before he flipped me around and pressed a piece of tape across my mouth, winding it around my neck and my hair in a double thickness.

He grabbed my arm and dragged me toward the back of the truck, where he used his other hand to lift the lever that secured the doors. "You better be wrong," he said grimly. "Otherwise you're going to rot in here."

He lifted me off my feet and pushed me inside. I landed hard on the floor, and before I could even struggle to my knees I heard the metal door slam and the security lever screech down, leaving me alone in the dark.

CHAPTER FIFTEEN

I struggled to my feet, nostrils desperately sucking in air that felt like a blast furnace and smelled like oil and sawdust. I waited for my eyes to adjust to the dark, but even then I saw nothing, no shapes or shadows; just flat gray-black desert-hot air.

It had to be a hundred ten, maybe a hundred twenty degrees inside the metal container. With no air circulation it felt even hotter. I would not survive here long. I had to find a way out.

I knew that the biggest mistake victims of life-threatening situations made was to panic. The hiker lost in the woods who wanders aimlessly until exhaustion and dehydration do him in. The driver of the car that goes underwater who uses up all her strength trying to escape the car before even determining which way the surface is. The victim of the house fire who desperately runs toward the nearest door and dies of smoke inhalation before he reaches it. Panic kills. I knew that. And I also understood for the first time what a powerful, seductive killer it was.

I wanted to plunge blindly into the dark in search of the exit, and I had to fight back the useless, pitiful screams that tried to rise in my throat. No sound I could make would be heard through the muffling layers of tape, and if I gave in to panic and started stumbling around in this heat I would only use up energy and become hopelessly disoriented. I forced myself to stand still, to breathe slowly, to think.

I tried to remember which way I'd been facing when I was pushed in here, which way I had turned when I stood up. I tried to envision how many steps I was from the door. Then I tried to picture the truck in my head. How many feet wide? How many feet long? The pulsing of terror in my ears slowed, and the breaths I took no longer burned my lungs.

I turned and walked forward. Five steps, six. All I could see was thick gray air. I felt the panic start to rise again. And then I slammed into something hard. It made a dull metal *thunk* when I hit it. I didn't know whether it was the door or a wall, but I turned my shoulder to it and hit it again. I leaned back a step and threw my weight forward, hitting it again, and again. Sweat soaked my hair and dripped into my eyes and the hot dry air that I dragged into my lungs scratched at my throat, returning too fast with a wheezing exhale. I pounded at the metal until I couldn't feel my shoulder anymore and then I turned and used the other one. I didn't really expect to make any progress toward escape, but if anyone passed by surely they would hear me. Surely.

I kept it up until I grew too dizzy and breathless to stand, and then I sank to the floor and used my feet to kick at the metal. My clothing was soaked now, my skin drenched. Bright sparks of light popped in front of my eyes. I had to stop and breathe.

I knew the police were looking for Sellers. If he took the time to search the weeds for my car keys, they might very well find him. If they did, if the police did search this part of the parking lot, the only way they would know I was here is if I kept making noise. And two golden retrievers running loose at the fair were bound to attract attention. Surely Marshall had noticed Cisco's escape, surely he had chased him here. If he had, he would hear me, of course he would. I just had to keep trying.

That's what I told myself as I tried to pull enough oxygen into my lungs to keep from passing out. But when, with a gargantuan effort, I lifted my feet again to pound against the door, I remembered that the direction which Cisco had chased the keys was on the other side of the parking lot from this truck; no one, looking for him, would pass this way. And all Sellers had to do was call Cameo to get both dogs to run to him; where Cameo went Cisco would follow. He might be gone with both of the dogs before Marshall, or the police, even thought to look here.

My strength was draining away in rivers of sweat. My skin was so hot it felt as though it was blistering. I had to rest.

My wrists were slippery inside their duct-taped ties, and I tried to wiggle them free, pushing out against the tape to stretch it, turning and pulling my wrists inside the too-tight bonds. It was no use.

Whatever give in the tape might have been created by my sweat and the heat was not enough. He had wrapped my wrists too tightly, and used too many layers. Duct tape was meant to withstand extremes of temperature and force. I tried for a while to loosen the tape around my mouth by rubbing my face against my shoulder. It might have worked if he hadn't wrapped the tape around my head more than once. As it was all I succeeded in doing was painfully ripping out a few strands of my hair.

Okay. I had to think. I couldn't keep on banging against the door like this; I was losing too much fluid and over-stressing my heart. Heat exhaustion was only moments away, if not already here. Heat rises, so the best thing I could do was to stay low, near the floor, and conserve energy. It was possible there might even be a loose seal near the door that would let in fresh air. Stay put. Stay still. Stay low.

Or get out of here.

What I needed was something sharp to cut the tape on my wrists. A shard of glass, a jagged piece of metal, a bolt or screw protruding from the wall that I could use to saw away at the tape. People did it all the time on television.

I pushed myself to my feet against the wall and kicked off my sandals so that I could sweep the floor with my bare feet for anything that might be useful. Inch by inch I made my way around the perimeter of the truck, pressing my hands and back against the wall to check for screws or nails or loose pieces of metal, sweeping my feet out in front of me along the dusty floor. I found some scraps of packing material, a crushed cardboard box, some cigarette butts, an empty paper cup. There were no nails, no broken bottles, no conveniently forgotten box cutter lying in a corner. By the time I returned to my starting place I was weak and light-headed, the heat pulsing around me like slow-boiling syrup. I was about to brace myself for the excruciating search of the middle of the floor, away from the safety of the walls, when my foot struck my shoe.

My shoe.

I dropped to a sitting position, pulling the sandal in to me with my toes and maneuvering myself around until I could grasp it with my fingers. Clumsily, I undid the buckle, dropping the shoe more than once and painstakingly picking it up again, until I held the loose strap between my fingers, buckle facing upward. I had to stop and rest, drawing in deep breaths through my flared nostrils. It took several tries, but I managed to position the buckle, with the prong held between my thumb and forefinger, against the bottom of the duct tape. I scraped the sharp point of the prong against the tape, trying to tear the fibers. Nothing. I tried again. And again.

It was only three o'clock in the afternoon. The hottest part of the day was still to come.

Time lost its meaning. I knew hours were passing only because I felt the heat building as the sun moved slowly, inexorably closer in the western sky. I worked at the tape with the little prong until my arms hurt so badly I could not make them move any longer. Then I rested for a while, and tried again. I thought I was making a little progress. Some of the bottom of the tape was beginning to fray, but as it did it became harder and harder to lift the buckle high enough to saw away at more fibers. I was dizzy, and I had to rest more and more often. The heat was searing.

For a time I tried to listen for signs of movement outside—voices, cars, police sirens. Dogs barking. Sometimes I thought I did hear those things and I would stop sawing at the tape and start kicking the door again, but then I began to worry I was hallucinating the sounds and I stopped wasting my strength. I could hear the sound of calliope music, muffled and far away, and sometimes the shriek of a happy fairgoer. But maybe I imagined that too.

My throat was like sandpaper, and I was so thirsty my stomach hurt. I didn't even know thirst could be like that, an ache that spread through every cell of your body. I thought about the liter bottle of water in my day bag. I thought about ice floating in the red-and-white striped soda cups they sold at the concession stand. I thought about paper cones filled with ice and drizzled with fruity syrup. Thinking about those things made me want to cry, but I didn't have any tears.

My wrists inside the tape weren't quite so slippery anymore. I wasn't sweating as much. And I remembered enough about heat exhaustion to know that was not a good sign.

I thought about white water rafting on the Nantahala River, and how the cold spray hits your face and drenches your arms when you steer into the rapids. I remembered how Buck and our friend Andy and I used to hike up the mountain as kids to a hidden spot in the woods and crawl out on the ledge overhanging a waterfall then cannonball into the pool below. It was crazy dangerous but, oh, that moment when the cold water shocks your sweaty body and then embraces it, the cool bright shower of the waterfall tumbling over your head and splashing off your shoulders … there's nothing like it in the world.

Funny how some things stay with you forever, just as sharp and real as the moment they first happened. I could almost taste that clear cold water, see the sun sparkle and glisten on the wet rocks, hear the roar of the falls. But Andy was dead, and Buck was married, and the three of us would never climb that waterfall together again.

And then the oddest thing happened. Somehow, deep inside I came to realize for the first time that it was okay. I still mourned for Andy, who had died too young, and I was sad for the loss of my marriage, which should have worked but hadn't. But that, like the childhood foolishness that allowed us to believe diving from the top of a waterfall was a good idea, was in the past now. It was over. And it was okay.

My head started to throb, and my neck grew so stiff I could barely move it. The shoe slipped from my fingers and I rested my head against the hot metal wall, focusing all my effort on breathing; just breathing. I tried to remember the symptoms of heat stroke, but I couldn't. All I knew was that when I closed my eyes to rest I saw swirling red lights and had crazy dreams about my skin frying on my body like bacon and then falling off in strips. I tried not to dream. I tried to keep my eyes open and think about cold things. Like snow. Last winter, when I'd been trapped in a blizzard up to my waist in snow I thought I'd had my fill. But now I clung to the memory of howling winds and ice-numbed fingers as though, if I thought about it hard enough, I could transport myself back there. It didn't work.

Cisco had saved me then, and everyone else on that mountain. Cisco, with the curiosity of a puppy and the heart of a hero, and Miles, who refused to give up on me even though I'd done everything in my power to make sure he did.

Cisco was still out there. He would find me. He was a search and rescue dog, after all. That was what he did. He would find me, of course he would, and he wouldn't give up until he did. All I had to do was hang on until he got here.

Miles was still out there too, and Melanie, and the unrealized future we might all have had together stretched out into the distance like the road not taken. Maybe that road was filled with pitfalls and dangerous curves and steep, twisty hills. But it was also filled with adventure and excitement and the thrill of possibility. I found myself desperately and unexpectedly hoping that Miles had not given up on me, either.

In the back of my head I heard Sonny saying, *I've never known anybody who worked as hard as you do for what you don't want.* But those days were over. Perhaps for the first time in a really long time, I actually knew what I wanted, and I was willing to fight for it.

I fumbled around on the floor for the shoe and positioned the buckle against the tape again. My fingers were stiff and aching and it was hard to make them work, but I started plucking at the tape with the prong again, catching fibers, pulling them away, gritting my teeth with the effort. It seemed I was making some progress this time, and when I pushed my hands apart, stretching out the tape, I actually felt it tear a little. I gripped the prong again, plucking and stretching, wiggling and tugging my hands inside their prison. And then, abruptly, one of my hands slipped free.

I was so surprised that I fell against the wall, chest heaving, eyes staring at absolutely nothing, for a single long moment unable to move. Then I tore away the tape from my face, and took a long gulp of thick, hot air, and another and another. I flung my hands against the metal but the sound it made was feeble and ineffectual. I tried to scream. All that came out was a croak.

I hit the wall again, and again. I sucked in hungry, wheezing, dragging gasps of air. My lungs were burning; my throat so dry that I couldn't even swallow. The rush and roar of my struggles for breath obscured every other sound, even the pathetically weak sound of my hands slapping against the metal. Every sound except one, and it was the most beautiful sound I'd ever heard.

It was the barking of a dog.

At first I thought I was hallucinating, and I stopped moving, stopped breathing, desperately trying to clear my head. Listening, heart pounding, lungs bursting, until it came again. The single, sharp bark of a dog.

"Cisco!" I cried, only no sound came out. My lips were too swollen to move, my throat too dry to make sound. But the joyous sound repeated over and over and over in my head as I pounded my hands on the wall, *Cisco! Cisco! Cisco!*

There was a mighty screech and the door against which I had been flinging myself fell open. I tumbled forward into sunshine and noise and swirling color and sweet fresh air. The last thing I saw was a blur of gold scrambling toward me; the last thing I felt before I sank into the cloud of unconsciousness was a sweet golden retriever licking my face.

CHAPTER SIXTEEN

I spent the next five hours in the emergency room hooked up to an IV drip. The first couple of hours were mostly a blur, punctuated by vivid dreams that featured, of all things, Cornelius S. Lancaster the Third. It was only after my head cleared and I regained enough strength to suck on ice chips that I began to realize those had not been dreams after all.

Corny's white, terrified face and shock of orange hair had been the first thing I saw when I regained consciousness on the stretcher before they put me in the ambulance, followed by Cisco's grinning face and two front paws on the sheet beside me. I saw him again as they wheeled me into the emergency room; he was trotting along beside me with Cisco's leash in his hand, shouting, "Out of the way, out of the way! This is a trained rescue dog!" Every time I opened my eyes over the next few hours, Corny was there, still wearing the dog-pin covered cap with tufts of frizzy hair sticking out from all sides, peering anxiously down at me, Cisco right beside him.

Now Cisco stretched out on the cool linoleum floor of my curtained cubicle while Corny brought me another cup of ice chips. Cisco was a familiar figure around the hospital, since he often did therapy visits here, but he had never been allowed in the emergency room before, and I couldn't imagine how Corny had gotten him in.

"Well," he admitted modestly, fluffing the pillow behind my head, "the police woman helped with that."

"Jolene?" I said, surprised.

He nodded vigorously. "Everyone was out looking for you. She even had her dog searching the woods, but of course you weren't there."

"It was Mr. Lancaster here who figured out how to find you." The male voice spoke from the entrance to the cubicle, and I looked around to see Marshall Decker hesitating there. "Is it all right if I come in?"

"Of course." I gestured him in with my free hand and tried to make sure I was decently covered in the flimsy hospital gown. "I'm sorry I dragged you into this," I added apologetically. "You were there, weren't you, when Cisco found me?" I thought I remembered seeing him but I really couldn't trust my memories from that time; everything was all jumbled up.

He nodded as he came over to me. "It took us a while to even realize you were missing," he admitted. "At first it was all about bringing down Sellers."

"You got him?" I said excitedly, pushing up onto my elbows. But the exclamation triggered a spasm of coughing, which made me dizzy, which resulted in a lot of fussing around on Corny's part and concerned looks from Marshall. Even Cisco got up from his nap to check on me.

"I'm okay," I gasped in a moment, waving my hand in front of my face as though to brush away the weakness. "I want to hear what happened."

Corny gave me a look of stern reprimand. "The doctor said you were to rest, and that we could only stay as long as you didn't get excited."

I said, "I won't. I promise."

Corny looked fierce enough to forcibly eject Marshall from the room if he caused any more trouble, and I hid a smile by lifting the cup of ice and tapping a few chips into my mouth. Marshall assured him, "I'll only stay a minute."

Corny relented and resumed his seat beside my bed. Cisco flopped down beside him with a sigh. I waited impatiently.

"Actually," Marshall said, "it was the dogs who're responsible for bringing down Sellers, although I probably could have been of more help if I had known what was really going on." Now it was his turn to look sternly at me.

"I guess I should have told you he had been there," I admitted uncomfortably, "and that the police were looking for him. I was just in such a hurry to get out of there, and I wasn't thinking clearly."

"I knew the police were looking for him," Marshall said. "I'm still a policeman myself, remember? But I didn't know he at the fairgrounds. When I'm elected sheriff," he told me, "there will be much more open communication between the police and the public."

I tried not to sigh out loud with impatience, but I must have, because he smiled a little and went on, "I felt so bad about letting your dog get away. I looked all over the fairgrounds for him. Finally somebody said they thought they had seen a dog running loose in the field behind the carousel so I headed that way and I spotted both of the dogs out in that field near the woods. I knew something was wrong because the last time I had seen the English Cream—what's her name?"

"Cameo," both Corny and I supplied.

"Right, Cameo. The last time I'd seen her she was with you, and I knew you wouldn't just leave a dog behind of your own free will. Then I saw Sellers, and I started after him. The stupid son of a—" His lips tightened and he finished grimly, "He took a shot at me. All right, I guess I was the one who was stupid, going after him like that without knowing whether or not he was armed. Anyway, he took off for the woods and I called the sheriff. They had what looked like a whole battalion there inside of forty-five seconds." His lips tightened briefly with a humorless smile. "That pretty little golden led the deputies right to him, with Cisco by her side."

I nodded. "She was crazy about him. She still thought of him as her dad." And my brows drew together as I said, "It's hard to think of him as a killer, when he was loved so much by a golden retriever."

"Dogs don't discriminate," Marshall said somberly, reminding me only of what I already knew. He added, "There might've been gunfire if it hadn't been for her. In fact, I'm pretty sure he would have tried to take out a few deputies before they took him, but he wouldn't risk hitting his dog."

"Maybe the judge will take that into consideration," I said, because, despite what he'd done, I couldn't believe anyone who loved a dog that much was entirely beyond redemption.

Marshall said harshly, "Don't start feeling too kindly disposed toward him. He was willing to let you die while he negotiated for a deal."

I shivered a little, and Corny reached over quickly to pull the sheet up around my shoulders.

"Of course they started a search right away," Marshall went on. "But they found your bag and your phone in the woods, so that's where the search was concentrated."

"He must've thrown them there," I said. "To hide the evidence. But you found my car keys, right?"

He nodded. "The K-9 unit did. We thought you must've dropped them. We searched that area too but didn't find anything to indicate what might've happened to you, and the K-9 couldn't pick up your trail. In a way that was a good thing. She's trained to scent blood and munitions. If she wasn't picking up either, we figured you were probably alive."

But all the while I was only a few hundred yards away, slowly smothering to death in a hundred-ten-degree metal box.

Marshall went on, "Of course Buck pulled out all the stops, called in two shifts to help with the search, and I think if it had gone on much longer his next move toward Sellers would not have been of the nonviolent type, if you know what I mean. I have a feeling our sheriff has a tendency to take certain things personally. Not," he couldn't resist pointing out, "a particularly good characteristic for an elected official.

"I decided to take the dogs back to your place so I could join the search," he went on, "and that's when Mr. Lancaster here demanded to know why Cisco wasn't searching. To tell the truth, I'd asked the sheriff the same thing, and he said Cisco wouldn't work without his handler, who was you. Deputy Smith concurred."

Corny, who had been practically bouncing on the edge of his seat throughout the telling, could restrain himself no longer. "They don't know how Cisco works," he confided to me earnestly. "If it had been a regular search, maybe they would be right. But Cisco *loves* you. He wasn't searching for a victim, he was searching for his *partner*. Of *course* he could find you!"

Marshall smiled. "He insisted on bringing Cisco back here and handling him himself. And sure enough, less than half an hour later Cisco led us to the truck."

Corny sat back in his chair, beaming. "Just like Lassie," he said.

I dropped my hand over the side of the bed, where Cisco's silky golden head rose to meet it. I stroked the plane of his skull, and closed my fingers gently around his ear. "Thank you," I told him, and he gazed up at me with his goofy golden retriever grin as if to say, *No problem.* I couldn't help grinning back.

"And thank you," I said to the two men. "Both of you."

Marshall inclined his head graciously. "Just a small sample of the kind of service you can expect when—"

"You're elected sheriff," I finished for him. "I know. And I'm still not working on your campaign."

He grinned. "Too bad. I'd already planned to order new posters with a picture of me and Cisco on them."

"People vote for animal lovers," I agreed.

He said, sobering a little, "I'm glad everything turned out okay. I'll let you get some rest." But just before he left he looked back. "It's a shame about the golden retriever. What do you think is going to happen to her?"

I looked at Corny. He tilted his head slightly and looked speculatively back at me. "I'm not sure," I replied thoughtfully. "I'll let you know."

The nurse came in, glanced disapprovingly at Cisco, checked my vitals, and hung another bag of fluids. Corny stayed out of the way, bustling about with the ice bucket and water pitcher on the bedside tray, until she was gone. Then he looked at me, small tight lines of distress appearing between his brows. "Miss Stockton, I don't want to upset you," he began uncertainly. "This probably isn't the right time, but I need to tell you some things."

I said, "Corny, I thought you were involved in all this. You shouldn't have lied to me."

He looked both relieved and dismayed as he came back to the chair and sat down, his hands clasped between his knees. "I didn't want to lie," he told me earnestly. "I tried so hard not to. I didn't want you to think badly of me. I just ..." He sighed. "I wanted the job so badly." He looked at me hesitantly. "How did you find out?"

I said, "In the first place, I talked to Professor Rudolph."

He dropped his gaze, ashamed. "I hoped if I did a good enough job you wouldn't check my references. Not all of them anyway."

"In the second place," I went on, "I knew you'd been in my house when you said you hadn't been. I found one of the dog pins from your hat."

His hand fluttered uncertainly to his hat and the distress in his eyes only deepened. "It was the first night I got there," he admitted. "By the time I finished work it was too late to find a place to stay so I sneaked back after you closed up the kennel. I thought if I stayed in the back room just that one night you'd never know and no harm would be done … but you almost caught me when that guy tried to break in and you came outside. I didn't know what to do so I ran in the house and hid there until you got back, then sneaked out the back door." Again he sighed. "I must've left the door open, and that's how Cameo got out. I felt so bad about that."

Technically, of course, he hadn't lied about that one; I'd specifically asked him if he'd been in my house on Friday, and he hadn't been. As for Cameo … well, I was most likely the one who'd left the door open, but I decided to let him take the rap for that, just to teach him a lesson. To emphasize my point, I said, "Corny, I almost implicated you in a murder investigation. This is serious business."

His eyes were big behind the glasses. "Yes, ma'am, I know. I'll tell the police everything I know about the attempted break-in, and about seeing Cameo and her mom walking that night at the campground. I was going to do that anyway. I would never withhold evidence," he assured me fervently. "Never."

I nodded. "That's good. I want you to know I picked up your stuff this morning at the campground. It should still be in the back of my car." His face lit up with relief, and then fell dramatically when I added soberly, "But Corny, I can't have an assistant who lies to me."

The despair that flooded his eyes, after the relief of only a moment ago, was heartbreaking. But then he squared his shoulders and started to stand. "Yes, ma'am. I understand."

"Which is why," I went on firmly, "I'm promoting you to head groomer and general manager. It's a full-time position with a lot more responsibility, and I need someone who can live on site. I trust that won't be a problem?"

He looked at me as though I'd just offered him the keys to the Taj Mahal. "N-no, ma'am," he stammered. "Not a problem at all."

"I was thinking the back room of the kennel," I continued. "You can use the kitchen and the full bath next to it, and you'll be in charge of opening and closing every day. Long hours, and the pay isn't that great, but at least you'll have a short commute."

"It sounds," he said, still stammering, still looking at me in wonder and disbelief, "it sounds like just what I've been looking for."

I smiled. "Me, too."

He rushed forward and embraced me awkwardly in the hospital bed, careful of the IV tube and the ice cup, exclaiming, "Oh, Miss Stockton! Thank you!

Thank you so much! You won't regret it, I promise
you that! I won't let you down! I'll be the best
employee you ever had! I'll treat your dogs like my
own! I'll ..."

"I know you will, Corny," I assured him, trying, a
little uncomfortably, to extricate myself. "And," I
reminded him firmly as he straightened up, beaming,
"you'll never lie to me again. About anything."

"I promise!" he declared, raising his right hand
solemnly. "My life is an open book. I have no secrets.
Ask me anything. I'm as transparent as glass. I ..."

Suddenly Cisco scrambled to his feet and raced
across the room, panting happily. I knew before I
looked around who had just entered.

Cisco flung himself on Buck, and Buck, smiling,
scratched Cisco's ears and ruffled his fur. I could not
help thinking, with an odd little stab of pathos, about
Cameo and Greg Sellers. And about Melanie and
Miles, and the woman who was trying to tear them
apart. Divorce had so many victims, so much fallout,
so many unintended consequences. And while it
rarely ended in murder, oftentimes the pain it caused
the innocent was as severe as if it had.

Cisco lowered his feet to the floor, claws clacking,
and Buck looked at me. He said, "You're looking
better."

Corny stood protectively between Buck and me,
his stance suggesting that if I but gave the word he
would gladly fly into battle for my sake. I had to
repress a smile.

"Buck," I said, "This is Cornelius Lancaster, my
new general manager at Dog Daze. Corny, Sheriff
Lawson."

Buck nodded politely. "Pleasure."

Corny said stiffly, "Sir."

"You were a big help out there," Buck added.

Corny was unmoved, remembering, no doubt, that the last time he had seen this man I had struck him in the face. My enemies were his enemies. I rather liked that, even though it might be a little inappropriate right now.

I said, "Corny, do you think you could get me some more ice?"

The ice bucket was almost full, but he took the hint, however reluctantly. "I'll just be a minute," he said, picking up the ice bucket. He moved past Buck with a look that on anyone else might have been construed as dark.

Buck came over to me, a large brown envelope in his hand. Cisco followed him adoringly. "Here are your things. Your keys, your phone, some dog stuff. We kept the duct tape as evidence."

I took the envelope. "Thanks."

"I'll send someone over in the morning to take your statement, but we've got enough on Sellers already to keep his lawyer busy for a while as it is. Kidnapping, assault on an officer with a deadly weapon, and, as soon as the ballistics report comes back on his gun, the murder of Tony Madison. Not to mention stalking and invasion of privacy. And that's just the top of the hit parade. Of course," he added, "our case would be a lot stronger if we could find that transmitter."

I said thoughtfully, "I might be able to help you out with that." He looked at me with interest and I said, "I have an idea. I'll let you know tomorrow.

Sellers said he didn't kill his ex-wife," I added. "He said he saw Madison do it."

Buck gave a small lift of his shoulder. "That's for a court of law to decide. I wouldn't be surprised if he was telling the truth on that, though. From what we were able to dig up, that Madison was a pretty nasty guy. Three wives died under mysterious circumstances before this one, but there was never enough evidence to bring to trial. That's why we were keeping such a close watch on him in the first place."

I should have known the sheriff's department had the investigation well in hand, even without my help. Buck knew how to run a case. And Jolene wasn't bad, either.

A brief silence fell, which Buck broke before it became too awkward. "Ro and Mart are here," he said. "They were in to see you earlier, but you probably don't remember. Mart says she's going to take you home with her for the night."

"I'd really rather go home and see my dogs."

"I told her you'd say that."

He bent to rub Cisco's ears one last time, then turned toward the door. "Well," he said. "I'm glad you're okay."

I had to hold Cisco's collar to keep him from following.

I said, "Buck."

He looked back.

"I'm sorry I hit you." I drew a breath and added, because I really meant it, "I hope things work out for you."

After a moment he smiled, although it seemed a little sad. "I hope things work out for you too, Raine. I really do."

When he was gone I reached into the envelope and pulled out my phone. I hesitated a moment, not because I was uncertain, but because I knew what I was about to do would change the course of my life. Or at least I hoped it would.

I got voice mail, but that was okay. I waited for the tone, and said, "Miles, hey, it's me. Listen, there's something I need to say to you."

CHAPTER SEVENTEEN

"**W**here was it?" Jolene demanded when I handed the small round disk over to her the next morning.

"In the lining of my purse. I thought I was putting it in a safe place when I put it in the zipper pocket," I explained, "but I forgot I used to keep dog treats there too. The dogs had chewed a hole in the pocket, and the transmitter fell behind the lining." Just like Corny's schnauzer pin, which I'd already returned to him, had done. I added, "In a way, I guess it *was* a safe place. If it hadn't gotten lost behind the lining, Sellers would have stolen it when he took my purse."

A corner of Jolene's mouth turned down dryly. "Dog treats?"

I shrugged. "It's what I do."

She sealed the little disc into an evidence bag and we walked out on to the porch. She had taken my official statement already, and told me that the preliminary ballistics report had shown that the bullet that had killed Madison came from Sellers's gun. She had also talked to Corny, whose information about having seen Cameo and April getting into a car Tuesday night only confirmed Sellers's story. It was starting to look as though Sellers might have been telling the truth about what happened to April, not that that made him any less guilty of subsequent crimes.

"It's kind of sad, isn't it?" I said as we stepped out onto the shade of the porch. It actually felt a little cooler today, although that might have been just me. After the three hours I'd spent locked in that truck I didn't think I would ever complain about the heat again.

Jolene cast me an inquiring glance and I explained, "Sellers had a good idea with the transmitter. He might have nailed Madison, might even have saved April's life. Even after April was found, if he'd just turned himself in and told you what he'd seen you could have arrested Madison before he even left the hospital. But he had to take the law into his own hands. Now the woman he loved is dead and he's going to prison."

Jolene murmured, "There's a lesson in that, Stockton."

I returned a dour look. "I have never," I informed her, "taken the law into my own hands."

It was Sunday afternoon, and the kennel was officially closed until five-o'clock pickup. I had given Corny the day off, but his idea of a day off was to set up the wading pools in the play yard and take the dogs out for a swim. I couldn't help grinning as I watched Cisco, with a chartreuse foam Noodle in his mouth that was twice his size, chase Cameo around the yard. Pepper splashed from pool to pool, trying to keep up with the fun, but was continually distracted by the floating toys she found there. Corny tossed a flying disc for Mischief while Magic lounged shamelessly in three inches of water. I had never seen any of them happier. This was going to work out just fine.

Jolene reached into her pocket and took out a citation book. My grin faded as she tore off a sheet and presented it to me wordlessly.

"Are you kidding me?" I stared at her incredulously. "You're giving me a *ticket*? For what?"

"Take it," she said impatiently.

I snatched the ticket from her and glanced at it. There was nothing written there but a name and a telephone number. I looked at her uncertainly, puzzled.

She glanced away, trying to hide embarrassment. "It's a doctor in Asheville," she said gruffly. "He's pretty good with PTSD. He might be able to help you with those nightmares."

My irritation dissolved, and when it was gone I didn't know what to feel. "Thanks," I said in a moment, a little awkwardly. I folded the paper and put it in my pocket.

Her lips compressed, as though she were tasting something bitter, and she looked back at me. "You were right about your dog," she said. "Nike is trained in law enforcement, not wilderness search. Cisco out-did her both times. I was thinking ... maybe it wouldn't be such a bad thing if the sheriff's department called on you from time to time. Unofficially, of course," she added quickly.

"Of course," I agreed, trying to keep a straight face.

"And with a clear division of labor."

I nodded. "I wouldn't have it any other way."

"And," she added severely, "this doesn't mean you've got free rein to go butting in where you don't belong."

"No chance," I assured her. "None at all."

She tried to stare me down. I just stared back. Then she muttered, "I've got to get back to work."

She started down the steps.

"Hey," I said.

She looked back, and I couldn't resist. I made the sign for a telephone with my thumb and pinky held to my ear. "Call me," I invited. "We'll have lunch."

For a moment she stood there, looking thoughtful, and then she said, "Maybe I will."

My jaw must have dropped, because she burst into laughter. I think it was the first time I'd ever seen her laugh. "Not in this lifetime, Stockton," she said, and I thought her step was particularly jaunty as she continued down the steps to her car.

By mid-afternoon Corny had shampooed and blow-dried Cameo, polished up her pink rhinestone collar, trimmed her nails and brushed her teeth, and had her looking her very best for the trip to her new home—which, fortunately for Cisco, was not very far away. Don't think I didn't agonize over the decision to let her go, both for Cisco's sake and my own. But part of being in the dog rescue business is learning to put the welfare of the dog before your own, and sometimes before that of someone you love. And when I saw the look on Marshall Decker's face as he knelt to hug Cameo, and the way Cameo grinned back at him, I knew I'd done the right thing.

"He needed her more than we did," I told Cisco as we watched them drive away. "And Cameo needed to be somebody's princess."

I sat on the porch with my feet on the top step, Cisco lying beside me with his head between his paws. I rested my hand on his neck, fingers entwined in his fur. "It's not as though we'll never see her again," I went on. "Marshall promised to bring her for play dates, and whenever he has to be out of town she'll stay with us. And if he's elected sheriff, she'll be at the office all the time. We can see her anytime we're in town."

Cisco just sighed. He definitely was not going to make this easy for me.

"You've got to think of what's best for Cameo," I said. "She's been through a rough time. She just lost the two people she loved most in the world, and she needs someone who can help her get through that. And, Cisco." I looked at him sympathetically. "I don't know how to tell you this, but she just wasn't that into you."

Cisco lifted his ears and turned his head toward me, making me think for one surprised moment that he'd actually been listening. But it was only Corny, coming up from the kennel with a freshly groomed

Pepper on lead. She was looking good and prancing high with a colorful tug toy in her mouth, occasionally pausing to give it a shake or toss it up in the air. Cisco got to his feet alertly, watching her.

"Three down, two to go," Corny said cheerfully, referring to the dogs who, after a morning spent splashing in the pools and chasing each other around the yard, had all needed baths.

I got up to take Pepper's leash. "I could help," I said. "It won't kill me to hold a blow-dryer and a slicker brush."

"Don't be sil! My job, my pleasure! You don't lift a finger until you're fully recovered. Can I bring you some more lemonade? Are you sure you wouldn't rather be lying down in the air-conditioning?"

I knew that level of solicitousness would get old fairly quickly, but for right now I was fine with it. To tell the truth, I could use a little pampering, and he did make great lemonade.

"Thanks, Corny, I'm good for now." I reached to put the gate in place across the porch steps, but he darted in front of me to do it himself. Like I said, it's nice to be pampered.

Cisco watched with waving tail as I unclipped Pepper's leash and she bounced across the porch, waving her toy gaily. When I released Cisco's leash he dashed after her, nipping at her tail feathers and then whirling into a play bow. She tossed the toy up into the air and he caught it. The next thing I knew they were playing tug like the old friends they were.

"Men," I murmured with a wry grin, "are so fickle."

Both Corny and I turned our heads at the sound of tires coming up the driveway. The car was an unfamiliar white sedan, and Corny said, "That must be an early pickup. I'll take care of it. Honestly, what part of 'no pickups before five' do these people not understand?"

He started to move the gate and go down the stairs, clucking his tongue reprovingly at the impudence of the early arrival. But the car did not turn toward the kennel, and as it drew closer, I thought I recognized the driver.

"That looks like a rental car," I said. "I don't think it's a customer. I think ..." I squinted my eyes against the sun for a better look, and my breath caught a little. "I think that's Miles."

Corny looked at me with lifted eyebrow. "Do we like him?"

The car drew to a stop and the passenger door flew open, discharging a young girl with tangled dark curls wearing a sequined tee shirt depicting the skyline of Rio de Janeiro. I knew that because "Rio de Janeiro" was written in sequined scroll across the top of the shirt. "Hey, Raine!" Melanie called. "We're home!"

A smile spread slowly over my face as the driver's door opened and Miles got out. "Yes," I answered Corny softly. "We do."

Miles closed the car door and stood there for a moment, looking rumpled and travel-worn in jeans, sunglasses, and a two-day growth of beard, and oh-so-good to me.

Corny glanced at me, then lifted his glasses to peer more closely at Miles. "Good choice," he murmured appreciatively.

He moved the gate as Melanie raced up the steps and flung herself into my waiting embrace. Nothing had ever felt better than that kid's hug, ever.

"Hello," Corny greeted her when she stepped away.

Melanie did a brief double take, returned an uncertain, "Hi." And before I could introduce them she caught sight of her dog. "Pepper!" she cried joyfully, and ran across the porch to embrace her. The two of them fell into a happy tangle, with Cisco adding to the celebration with a few excited barks. My smile turned into a full-fledged grin.

"I'll be in the kennel," Corny said, holding the gate for me, "if you need me." And, as I went down the steps toward Miles, he added, "Somehow I don't think you will."

I stood uncertainly in front of Miles. With his eyes obscured by the sunglasses I couldn't tell much about his expression at all. I said, "Hey."

He let a beat or two pass. Then he said, "I had the strangest voice mail as we were landing in Miami. It was from someone who sounded a lot like you, but she was saying things I never thought I'd hear come out of your mouth. So I thought I'd better drive up and make sure you were okay. That you hadn't been abducted by space aliens or suffered a concussion of some monumental degree, because with you anything is possible." He looked me up and down and added, "Looks like a good thing I did, too. What did you do to your knee?"

I replied with a shrug. "Just a little tussle with space aliens. Nothing serious. Bruised, not broken." Then, "You didn't really drive up from Miami."

"Atlanta," he replied, and waited.

I tilted my head a little, trying to discern some hint of his mood behind the glasses. "This person who sounded like me, what did she say?"

"Oh, something outrageous about being in love with me. Can you believe that?"

I nodded slowly. "I can," I whispered.

I reached up and took off his sunglasses. His eyes were deep and thoughtful and silver gray, waiting patiently for me, as he so often did. I said, "I do love you, Miles, and I love Melanie. The only reason it took me so long to say that is because I was afraid it would hurt too much if I lost you. And maybe I will lose you. Maybe it won't work out for us. But if it doesn't, I don't want it to be because I didn't try. I'm better when I'm with you, Miles, and I think you're better with me. Maybe not in every way, but in all the ones that count. And ..." I drew a breath, searching those quiet, kind, and patient eyes. "If I'm the reason you're in a custody battle now, then it's only right that I should stay and help you fight. If you want me," I added, with the just the smallest note of uncertainty in my voice.

Miles drew me gently into a long and slow embrace, resting his chin atop my hair, just holding me. "I want you," he said simply.

I thought I could have stood there forever, content and at peace for the first time in what felt like years. Then Melanie called from the porch, "Hey, Raine! You didn't see my earrings!"

I smiled and stepped away from Miles. He smiled back. "It's good to be home, sweetheart," he said.

"Yeah," I agreed. "It's good to have you home."

"Raine!" Melanie called impatiently.

Miles slipped his arm around my waist as we walked back to the house. "Anything interesting happen while I was gone?" he asked.

"Not much." I leaned my head against his shoulder. "I hired a new guy for the kennel."

"Good for you."

"I placed a rescue dog," I added, in the interest of full disclosure. "And Cisco and I went on a search."

"Did you?" He glanced down at me with interest. "You'll have to tell me all about it."

And I would, someday. But right now Melanie was waiting, and I had more important things to do.

ABOUT THE AUTHOR….

Donna Ball is the author of over a hundred novels under several different pseudonyms in a variety of genres that include romance, mystery, suspense, paranormal, western adventure, historical and women's fiction. Recent popular series include the Ladybug Farm series, the Hummingbird House series, the Dogleg Island Mystery series and the Raine Stockton Dog Mystery series. Donna is an avid dog lover and her dogs have won numerous titles for agility, obedience and canine musical freestyle. She divides her time between the Blue Ridge mountains and the east coast of Florida. You can contact her at http://www.donnaball.net.